M000295507

For Hire: Audition

By

Kevin A. Patterson

&

Alana Phelan

A For Hire Enterprises Publication

Cover Art by IG: Therabeth
Editor: Angela Smith
Consultants: Cassandra Klinepeter & Imani Thomas

ISBN: 978-1-7328728-3-7

Code: 001

To my best friends. I spent more hours than I can count chopping it up with y'all about geek shit. Thanks for keeping my imagination and creativity sparked. More than that, thanks or being the realest people I know. Your honesty keeps me honest.

Kev

To Aimee, my Glamazon, for her strength and vulnerability, her support and advice, and her ability to kill off a container of salsa with me with no regrets

Alana

For Hire: Audition

"Of course, nobody knew it was happening while it was happening. It was only in hindsight you could see the combination of people and events leading us to where we are now. You had Franklin Curry in the summer of 1968. He made social justice and superhero work a joint crusade. A year later, you had the Stonewall Riots and that really kicked off the LGBT movement. The point where those two things really crossed paths in a major way, specifically for trans people, was in 1976 with Mors Maldonado, the hero called El Peligro. When he was misgendered and called his old hero name by a politician giving him an award for heroism, he took decisive action with one punch. It launched a nationwide conversation about how we treat and respect transgender folks. It was just a single punch, but it changed laws, introduced protections, and revolutionized both language use and medical access. Two decades later, most trans kids only really know Peligro from the one good photo taken during the altercation. But without that one punch, who knows what the world would look like?"

Historian Dr. Carly Steif — For Hire *magazine* — October 1998

Chapter 1

Vanessa

I'm really gonna miss this, I thought as I woke up in Elise's arms. She was so warm that it made the rest of the world feel cold by comparison.

It wasn't just her body, either. She was kind and giving and amazing. She was twenty-five, only three years older than me, but she already worked as an aide for a law firm handling pro bono cases for the underprivileged citizens of our hometown, Cargill, New Jersey. She volunteered at the community gardens and always brought home fresh vegetables to cook into spectacular meals for her unending parade of friends. She had her shit together, and if she could, she'd have made an honest go at a serious relationship with me. That's why it had to end.

I didn't need to walk away, but I was about to. For both our sakes.

We'd been together for months and she paid for all our dates because she knew I couldn't afford to. How long before she felt like I was taking advantage of her? How long before that understanding look in her eyes turned to pity or, worse, disgust? She was about to become

4

a lawyer and I was a barista with no further prospects. How long before she got annoyed by my lack of direction?

As someone born with Genetic Variance Syndrome, I could tell you exactly how long. That was my power: I could figure the outcome easy as breathing. Everyone thinks my power is fake or tainted by my own feelings, but there were lots of variables at play and my mind never stopped calculating. Elise and I, basketball was our thing. Unlike me, she still played at the rec center. At some point in the next few months, she was going to see an artifact from my playing days and ask me why I stopped. That baggage would drag us down. I didn't want to be responsible for tainting her shit with my own. Best to go out on a high note.

Instead of the slow path to disintegration, I'd just sneak out of the spacious apartment that I could never afford half the rent on and ghost. But before that, I had to say goodbye. Not to Elise, who could only wake up to a screeching alarm, thank god. I had to say goodbye to Gizmo, her huge rough collie, my true love and heartbreak. We met during a lunch break at the local dog park and it was mutual adoration at first sight. His human was nice enough to converse with, and it progressed from there.

Honestly, this was a better system for me: Pet the dog, bang the human, pet the dog again, then leave. No domestic fantasies here. I had nothing to offer.

I slid out of Elise's bed, kissed her lightly on the forehead, pulled my dress on over my head, and left the bedroom as quietly as possible. Every noise echoed in the cavernous space and might give me away. I didn't want to mess this up. Let her sleep in. Let her dream.

I took my last looks as I walked through. It was always so spotless here, but I guess it didn't take much to clean an apartment that only held a few beautiful pieces of art, a large couch, and a huge television. I'd miss the TV too. It was the best for watching the Cargill Gizmos' star point guard "Break-of-" Dawn Taylor while curled up next to the team's namesake.

It was like he was waiting for a game night now, napping in his usual spot. I paused to hug him. He opened his eyes, yawned, and licked the side of my face. Unfortunately, it couldn't last as long as we both wanted. I was already running late. For someone who rarely had anywhere important to be, I was always running late.

"I'm gonna miss you, buddy," I whispered into his soft fur, then reluctantly got up. He put his head back down and shut his eyes, sure I'd be back. I blinked away some tears I wasn't expecting.

I hoped Elise would forgive me for ghosting. It was really for her own good. Same as with Adam and Rashmi and Malik—especially Malik. I was grateful for all the cute pet-parents I'd shared some time with, but it was better to leave too early than to stay too late.

Vanessa Copeland: Dog Lover, Escape Artist.

I carried my bike down the front stairs of the apartment building. It was quicker than the ramp and I needed all the shortcuts I could get. This was my favorite version of Cargill—the only people out this early were me and the delivery drivers bringing around fresh bread or newspapers. There was just enough sunshine and barely any traffic. I could listen to a few tunes and scan all the local businesses without worrying about distraction putting me in physical danger. It took only twenty minutes to ride to work.

I locked my bike to the rack in front of the coffee shop and walked in, steeling myself for the well-deserved, totally annoying, and ultimately harmless admonishment I had coming.

My spirits lifted slightly at the coffee aroma that hit me in the face when I opened the front door. Thank goodness for small pleasures. I'd dated people who worked in much less friendly-smelling environments and was glad I didn't leave work every day smelling like gasoline or toner cartridges. As usual, though, that first pleasant moment upon entering JoMo Java was cut short by JoMo himself.

Joey Maurice was a short, stocky almost-local with bad skin and even worse hair. He didn't know how to talk to people or run a business that inspired employee loyalty. Almost none of his best workers stayed on for much longer than a year. I was in my eighth month. If I'd had anything better going on, I would've been out of there by the end of this sentence. But I didn't.

The one thing Joey knew—the thing that kept his business going despite himself—was how to make incredible coffee. His technical skill overshadowed all the interpersonal skills he lacked. Not even the former employees who'd studied his methods could successfully replicate them at their new locations. When the city magazines and websites gave their annual awards for the best coffee in Cargill, the list was packed with JoMo protegees. The guy that taught them all was always number one.

"Every day you're late, Van! Again today!" Joey was putting on the final pots of regular and decaf for those who wanted a standard drip. He didn't even turn to see me. I guess he was just used to the exact minute of my lateness. That was me, a consistent fuck-up.

7

"Nobody's in yet, Maury. I'll get the counters clean and floor swept before the rush gets poppin'." Every day went the same way: Clean the store. Serve the same customers at roughly the same times. Don't get fired. Don't quit. Clean the store again. Go home. Pay the unending flood of bills. Nothing ever changed in the life of Vanessa Copeland: Disaffected Barista. Until the day it did.

Chapter 2

Camille

Camille Baston was done with a lot of things. She was done with her job, done with being financially underwater, and, to a certain extent, done with her marriage. Unfortunately, these things were hopelessly linked. The only way to get away from the stress of her home life was to go to work. The only way to get away from the stress of her job was to go home. She wouldn't even look at the banking app on her phone. That would take her over the edge.

So, without the ability to be truly done with everything she was done with, Camille Baston chose to be done with this day in particular. Her late shifts as the superhero B-Girl almost always ended with a cup of coffee, her smallest piece of self-care. The caffeine kick allowed her to endure the few hours she spent arguing with her husband before sleeping through the afternoon and early evening.

JoMo Java had the best brew in town, but that's not why she went there. When B-Girl was a young and idealistic hero, she put away a thief she'd gone to high school with. A few years later, Joey Maurice got out of jail and tried to go back to stealing. Hoping to dissuade him from a life of crime, Camille beat him up but didn't arrest him. Two years after that, he was a successful small-business owner. Maybe she liked lording her influence over him, or maybe she just liked being reminded of a time when she knew she could make an impact. One way or the other, this was her coffee source.

A little bell tinkled as she walked in the door but Camille barely noticed it over the sound of her old classmate yelling.

"You're overpouring, Van! This is your fault. My accounting says I'm coming up short for the month. And I know it's because of you and your soft heart."

The young woman at the counter was still serving a line of customers as she took in this lecture. The kid had barely registered before but Camille was suddenly interested in seeing what she would do next. As the line drew Camille closer to the counter she really looked at her for the first time. Late teens, maybe early twenties. Taller than Camille had initially noticed. Her skin was a richer, deeper brown than Camille's own amber complexion, and her box braids were neatly tucked into a hairnet. Her expression was neutral but Camille saw her muttering under her breath when she turned away from the counter.

"Large nonfat latte, extra hot with caramel drizzle," she said when Camille was finally in front of her.

"That's right." It was a picky order, but then, Camille was an exacting person, if she did say so herself.

She stepped to the far end of the counter to wait for her drink. As the barista started on the order, moving smoothly through familiar motions, she finally responded to her manager. "You're not coming up short because of overpouring, *Joseph*." Camille grinned. This girl had some fire to her. "You took Alma and Corey off their closing shifts early last week and forced me to work a pair of doubles to cover. Both times pushed me into overtime, which overshot how much you *thought* you were saving by cutting them short, especially since I make eighty cents more hourly than Alma and sixty-three more than Corey. Then you took home a pound of Sumatra to wrap up as a gift for your mother-in-law.

"You screwed up the printing for the new flyers which cost you a whole ream of paper and a print cartridge. The prices went up on both of our sweetener brands just before we restocked because gas prices went up a couple months ago and you probably forgot to update the numbers. All in all, you're probably four hundred sixty-three dollars and twenty-eight cents off budget. Is that about right?"

Completed latte in hand, the barista turned to a wide-eyed Camille and plastered on a passable smile to hand her the drink. She went back to the register without missing a beat.

JoMo muttered something incomprehensible, stomped into the back office, and slammed the door shut behind him.

Some sort of idea began forming in Camille's mind. She wasn't quite sure what it was, but she knew it was going to start with this kid. She dropped a twenty and a magazine on the counter and said, "I'm taking this copy of *For Hire* too. Keep the rest for yourself." After a pause she added, "Thanks." She couldn't remember if she'd ever said it here before.

In another deviation from the norm, Camille, who always left the store immediately after receiving her drink, decided to stay. She pulled out a chair at the small table nearest to the counter and sat down in direct sight of the kid behind the register. The morning rush came and

11

went as Camille sat and read her copy of the country's most popular superhero magazine, trying to ignore the familiar pang when she didn't see herself mentioned. All the while, she cast occasional glances at the young woman behind the counter.

When the crowds thinned after rush hour, JoMo emerged from his office holding the store's ledger. "Look, Van," he said in an almost-apologetic voice. "You were right about the amount. You've been doing good work here but I'm paying you too much. If I'm gonna turn a profit, I gotta cut your hours."

"You already turn a profit," she replied with a smirk. "If you cut my hours any more than you already have, I'm not full time. I'd lose my insurance coverage. Estradiol doesn't pay for itself, you know. Don't be a dick."

"There's nothing I can do about that. The store's gotta turn a profit."

"The store already turns a profit," she repeated. "If you want to make more money, stop trying to get cute with Corey and Alma's hours and then paying me time-and-a-half to cover the difference. Stop taking home free product. If you had swapped out the cappuccino machine when I said so a few months ago, you could've sold the old one for double what you can sell it for now and you'd have saved almost six hundred dollars on last-second repairs that a new machine wouldn't have needed. Then you wouldn't be bothering me about overpouring. I can think of five more things, off the top of my head, that'll make you more in cost reduction than messing around with my hours. Give me the ledger and I can probably find more."

Camille watched as she grabbed a pencil from a cup full of them, snatched the ledger out of his hands, and began furiously scribbling in it. The gears in her head were turning; her ideas were forming into something coherent. Why was this kid's obvious talent being wasted making coffee? After another few minutes of pretending to read, and once JoMo had gone into the back, Camille got up and returned to the counter once more.

She didn't draw attention to herself, just reached into her purse (baby blue like the rest of her outfit) and felt around in it until she was noticed. The kid, Van, looked up, found the older woman directly in front of her, and took a step back. Camille's well-manicured hand emerged from the purse holding a business card. On it was a gold and diamond encrusted capital B on a pink background—a stylized version of the logo on her jumpsuit. She placed it on the counter and slid it towards Van with a single finger.

"You make good coffee but it seems like you ain't making good money. In fact, it sounds like JoMo is trying to short you the little bit he's even paying you. This weekend, call the number on the back of this card. I think I got something for you." She made her exit with a flourish, just how she liked it.

Chapter 3

Vanessa

You know that feeling where something happens and you don't know how to react to it in the moment but then you come up with the perfect response after it's already too late? I had just experienced the first part and was desperately hoping for the second one to arrive.

"Who was that customer in the jumpsuit? Extra hot with the caramel drizzle? She looks like a superhero." I handed JoMo back the ledger with my shiny new and highly accurate notes. Superheroes weren't really my jam. Some people thought it was weird how I wasn't into the whole thing, especially with me being a variant and all, but to me the superhero fandom felt like rewarding people just for being who they were. Which is why I could name the Gizmos' lineup for the past ten years without blinking an eye but I could only name a few superheroes by sight. Basketball, now that's where you had to put in the work.

"Her name's B-Girl," he said, with a familiar *you should know this* face. "We were classmates back in the day. After graduation though, she started doing that and I - uh - I started doing this. As heroes go, she's pretty old school."

Whatever that meant.

"I'm taking my break," I told him, and because he'd been hiding in the office all day and leaving me to serve everyone, he couldn't argue. I took off my apron, made myself a drink (which employees had to pay for, of course), and sat down at a table with my phone out.

Missed you this morning, the notifications read. *Talk to you later.*

If I were braver, I'd just tell Elise that I was going through a lot and couldn't see her anymore. But I wasn't. I cleared the notification, but I didn't delete the message.

Finding information on B-Girl was easy. The city of Cargill made a dossier available for each of its superhuman defenders, from the GVS-enhanced office staff all the way up to household names like Double M. The public records were pretty dry, though. They only contained a minimal biography and personal statistics for each superhuman listed: real name, code name, height, weight, age, years active, hometown, power ("body control"), and badge number—as if any superhero actually wore a physical badge on their uniform. I learned that B-Girl's full name was Camille Latonya Baston. She was fifty years old and she'd been active as a hero for thirty-two years. Thirty of those years were spent in Cargill after serving the first two in her nearby hometown of Hawkins.

To find anything more substantial, I had to go to the *For Hire* website. The magazine maintained a comprehensive database of each superhumans it had any information on. A search for B-Girl returned the same personal stats but also a series of media quotes, relevant articles, and endorsement deals, along with a record of deeds done—often accompanied by eyewitness videos. Even with all this information, the pickings felt slim. Thirty-two years should've meant a wealth of information on her, especially given that *For Hire* itself was about to reach its thirty-year anniversary, as every banner ad on the site blared.

In case my expectations were wrong about the lack of available details, I visited the Double M profile. Despite an active superhero career spanning less than a quarter of time time of B-Girl's, Marcella McKenzie's profile was an entire filing cabinet full of adventures and related media compared to the handful of loose-leaf sheets that made up B-Girl's profile. I went back to B-Girl's page and read in depth. Some of the sections, like relevant articles and endorsements, were almost bare. There were only a handful of links to news reports from the late 1990s and early 2000s. All were related to takedowns of the type of minor crimes that wouldn't have rated a TV appearance had they been overseen by non-powered law enforcement. There wasn't much indication of what B-Girl had been up to over the last ten to fifteen years. One had to assume more of the same, or maybe even less.

The lone endorsement deal was with the local apparel company that supplied her velour jumpsuits. But even that was for a ten-year contract signed almost thirty years ago. This deal was struck right when she transferred from her hometown to the big city, when she was up and coming. Her outfits were still crisp though. Either B-Girl maintained them extremely well or she had been paying out of pocket for years to maintain her signature look.

16

That was about it. I did a general search for her superhero name and ended up learning where she got it from. A "b-girl" was a type of street dancer stemming from the early days of hip-hop, back when my parents were still kids. "Centered around the block party culture of New York City," a website called *Flow House Redux* read, "DJs would loop the rhythm sections of disco and pop albums by switching back and forth between two turntables playing the same song. This formed the basis for hip-hop music, as the extended break sections allowed time for MCs to rap and for dancers to dance. The dancers took on the name break-boys and break-girls, shortened to b-boys and b-girls. It was clear that B-Girl had crafted her look as a tribute to that classic era of American culture. Or, as JoMo put it, "old school."

What did that have to do with her power? It said "body control" on both the city and *For Hire* sites, but there were no details and no camera phone footage. Did she... dance her enemies into submission? The article I read said the school of hip-hop that her clothing represented was "hypercompetitive." I imagined her challenging criminals to dance battles and arresting them when they lost. Which in my head was hilarious.

Nothing about the bare-bones information provided suggested what she was after. B-Girl seemed to be a superhero who never really hit her stride and was nearing the end of her career. What could she offer a twenty-two-year-old barista? One that, I reminded myself, she had ignored for eight months before today.

She'd heard me talk to JoMo, though. Maybe she wanted to use my powers for something. But I knew I wouldn't make a good superhero. My powers were subtle. Hell, my own dad didn't even believe in them unless he benefited from it.

Yeah, I needed money if I wanted to do more with my life, but all I really wanted was to watch basketball, play video games, and hug massive puppies. If whatever B-Girl wanted didn't lead to that outcome, it might as well be just another shitty barista job.

Thanks but no thanks, I thought, sliding my phone back into my bag and going to finish out the brief remainder of my shift.

Chapter 4

Camille

Camille walked into her home and almost tripped over a hammer. A wave of annoyance came over her, but she breathed it out. After all, she wasn't going to fall. She never fell.

Her husband Reynolds was on a stepladder removing a painting from above the fireplace. The painting was of her—not in her B-Girl costume, but in a deep red evening gown and lush faux-fur stole. She looked fierce and elegant. Darkness swirled behind her with the tiniest hint of gold.

"You're home a little late," he said over his shoulder.

"I posted up at JoMo's for a bit. There was a kid there who was really good with numbers. I'm gonna try to work wi– what the hell are you doing, Rey?"

"I found a buyer," Rey said, gently but firmly working the painting off its hooks. "More than what we paid for it." He was a big man but graceful, slow and deliberate. Camille didn't worry about the painting being damaged. That was literally the only thing she wasn't worried about.

"Is this necessary?" She set down the empty coffee cup with its tacky label and watched him descend, keeping her face blank.

Rey's smile dropped off his face. "We discussed this, Cammie. This sale will float us for a couple of months."

Her eyes never strayed from the painting. "Is that the last one?"

"Nah, there's still the Wiesenberg in the dining room."

Not that they ever ate in there anymore. The table had cost twice a mortgage payment, too.

Closing her eyes, she brought her hands to her temples, slowly rubbing in small circles to ward off a stress migraine. She could kill a man with her bare hands, her feet, or even her hair, but she couldn't manage what was happening inside her. If only the precision control she had over herself extended inward so she wouldn't have to deal with any of this: the money problems, Rey, the quiet. She could knock herself out and wake up after the nightmare that was her current week.

Was it actually quiet, though?

"What's that?"

Rey had set the painting down and was in the process of wrapping it, but Camille's words brought him stumbling to his feet. "I'm sorry, babe, let me just get that."

"What. Is. That."

"It's a little jazz, is all. I'll just—" He rushed out of the room and, blissfully, the sound cut off. Too little, too late. Camille followed him.

"Was that *him*?"

Their bedroom was bare now, too. The wall hangings, the statue on the dresser, gone. Half of Camille's jewelry, too. She kept the jewelry box closed now. It depressed her too much.

20

"I missed him," Rey said, dropping his eyes.

"Well, he's gone and pining isn't going to fix it," she snapped. She climbed into bed fully dressed, kicking her shoes off before tucking her feet under the plush down comforter. "I'm getting a migraine. Pull the drapes and go get rid of the last beautiful thing we got."

"The Wiesen—"

"Oh my god, Rey, just go!"

When the door clicked behind him, she breathed a sigh of relief. She could barely stand to be around him right now. No one ever told you when you loved two men that when one left, the one who remained would be a constant reminder of the one who didn't.

Mateo, she thought, and then immediately tried to shut the thought of him out of her head. She tried to focus on the plan, but the migraine kept her from focusing at all.

The door opened again.

"Reynolds Baston—"

"Baby, I brought you your meds. And a glass of water."

She shut her mouth and looked at the man who'd been part of her life since she was a teenager. He was as handsome as he'd ever been. He had made her feel tiny and delicate, precious, for more years than she wanted to admit.

He put the pill bottle and glass on her bedside table and dutifully went to pull the drapes.

God, he was too good for her. She was too good for him. It depended on the time of day.

"I'm sorry, baby," she told him in a low voice. "I was up past my bedtime and it made me crabby." He walked over to her hesitantly and she reached out for his hand, bringing it to her face. "You always take care of me."

"I always will. I love you, Cammie."

"Love you, Rey." She reached over and took one pill, considered taking a second but decided against it.

"You want me to rest with you?"

"Yeah," she said after a pause. "Yeah, baby, I do."

He got into his side of the bed and enveloped her. The bed was too big for just the two of them now, so they pretended it wasn't by staying as close as possible. The space was a reminder neither of them wanted, so they spooned facing away from it, always. It was unspoken. It was necessary.

Camille shut her eyes, hoping the meds worked faster than the headache, or that sleep would take her first. She matched her breathing to Rey's. She could think about the plan later.

The world went black.

Chapter 5

Vanessa

The thing about failing to reach your goals is that a million little things were there to remind you it never happened. Whether that was putting on an apron with a coffee store logo instead of a basketball jersey every day, a steadily-decreasing number of unanswered texts on your phone, or just That Look in your dad's eyes when you came back to your childhood home every day.

"Van?" he called from the kitchen the moment I opened the door. Sometimes I wondered if he had super-hearing. But what kid didn't think that about their parents? The smell of popcorn was unmistakable. I continued back into the kitchen and saw him pull a fresh bowl out of the microwave and place it on a tray next to a glass of wine—his nightly snack. He was wearing a robe over pajama pants and a t-shirt from his alma mater. I'd covet the Gizmos socks he wore if he didn't pair them with sandals, thus turning me off them forever. Vance Copeland, Sr. may have been a moderately successful businessman out in the world, but at home he was just my dorky dad. "You're in kind of late. JoMo force you into another double shift?"

"Nah," I lied. "Someone called in sick and I volunteered to cover." Sometimes... I mean, usually... fine, I *always* wanted him to believe that I had a better work ethic than I really did, that I was still High School Vanessa or even College Vanessa. There were days where he'd clap me on the back and praise my fake effort. Not today, though.

"You know," he said, angling his nose to the ground so he could look at me over the top of his reading glasses, "Tax season isn't really over. With the extensions and all, I mean. There are still people who could use your help."

I'm gonna pause for a second to say that my relationship with my dad was complicated. He'd always been a good father and I'd usually been a fantastic daughter, but he hadn't always seen me and that caused friction. Case in point, my dad had tried no less than two dozen times in the previous eight months to get me out of the coffee shop and into an entry-level accounting job. A job that did not give benefits, was only seasonal, and guaranteed nothing, by the way. But I guess accounting sounded less disappointing than food service.

That would be an average of roughly once every week and a half, if you did the math, and of course I couldn't *not* do the math. Imagine if someone annoyed you the same exact way about every ten days. Now imagine if you lived with and were financially beholden to that person. That was another way failing to reach your goals sucked: you ended up beholden.

"Thanks, Dad. I've got my own prospects," I lied again, pretty much for the same reason I lied last time. "When they materialize into something more solid, I'll let you know."

He let the point drop this time. Had he pushed it further, it might have started a fight. I was glad it didn't. I loved my dad but he always wanted me to be something I wasn't. He thought I should've been an accountant, but instead I was a really good barista. He thought I could've been a small forward, but I ended up as a versatile point guard. He expected me to be a son but—oops!—he got a daughter.

And that's why I spent my life lying to him. Now it was about telling him I had job prospects that I really didn't. Back in high school, I'd show off my unusually high rebounding stats and talk up how positionless basketball was the way of the future. I'd let him call me "Van" and himself "Senior." Little lies like that gave him hope and gave me a supportive father.

After the events of today, I wondered how he'd feel if I were a superhero. I mean, I couldn't dance criminals into submission, but I was sure the local PD could find a way to exploit my abilities. That is, if I was okay with throwing myself into danger—or bureaucracy. I wasn't thrilled with the idea of either, to be honest.

I headed upstairs to relax a bit before crashing. Between the pseudo-job offer from the hero and the frankly naive job offer from my dad, I was done with this day. I usually went to bed in just my underwear but I was feeling a little colder than usual. Since I didn't have Elise to curl up next to, I went for the next best thing: my fuzzy pajamas and my Dawn Taylor T-shirt. It was the height of comfort as I turned on my Mochia FunBox and got under the covers.

I was exhausted, but I could squeeze in a couple of multiplayer matches of my current favorite game, *The Partition*, before I drifted off. I followed my set routine of turning on the TV and setting the sleep timer to one hour. It was a way of forcing myself to eventually put down the controller and call it a night. I was about to hit the input button on the remote control when I noticed what was showing on live TV.

On the screen sat that talk show host Shae Livingston, wearing a sharp suit and a huge smile. She was behind her desk, holding her cup, and bobbing her head as her in-studio band ended their musical intro. My game console was on, but I could at least see who her first guest was before I switched over to the game. It might have been Dawn Taylor talking about the remainder of the season and the potential playoff matchup against Miami. You never know.

"Returning for her fourth appearance, *For Hire*'s number one superhero for *twenty! seven! months! straight!* The lovely! The invincible! Double M!"

Are you kidding me? It was like the day had a theme, and that theme was local superheroes.

The most popular one of all came striding out from backstage, all purple hair, warm brilliant smile, and confident strength. She blew a kiss to the in-studio band and waved to her legion of fans. She wore an amazing dress that had a corset top covered in blue, pink, and purple sequins, with a skirt that was soft and loose and hit her mid-thigh. I sighed, but I didn't know which I coveted more: the dress or the woman. The crowd really ate it up, too.

Even with my minimal knowledge of superheroes, this was who I thought of whenever anyone mentioned the term. There were maybe five or six that I could recognize, and that list now included B-Girl. Double M was only one of two superheroes I even came close to caring about—the other, of course, being the trans hero, El Peligro. The 1976

26

photo of him punching out a politician for misgendering him was legendary.

In the here and now, though, Double M's popularity was unavoidable. Products with her name and face were available everywhere. Every newsstand held fashion magazines with her on the cover. Videos of her heroism were a constant fixture on my social media feeds whether I wanted them or not. On everyone's, really.

This put the whole B-Girl encounter into perspective. They were such opposite ends of the spectrum. I wondered if I would have been less skeptical and more receptive if it had been Double M that handed me a business card. Who am I kidding? Of course I would have been.

It seemed that the women on the television heard my thoughts as I let the controller fall out of my hand and settled in to watch for a bit, my eyelids surprisingly heavy.

"See, the superhero culture is hyper-competitive," Double M said when asked about her upcoming training program. "When I first got started as a hero, a lot of the active leaders on the power rankings were really hard on me. I don't know if it was my age, or my talents, or my hair. But a lot of the top dogs just didn't like me." The crowd began to boo and the superstar held up her hands to calm them. "No, no, no. It's okay. It's fine. Times are hard, and we've got a stressful job. These were all brave and honorable heroes. But not everybody has the time or the patience to be polite to the bright-eyed new kid."

I never heard the TV shut off. I drifted off into a dream where I was sporting a blue velour jumpsuit with a Gizmos logo on the front. Even asleep, I couldn't get away from superheroes. But I have to admit it was a pretty cool dream.

Chapter 6

Camille

"Dispatch, what you got for me?" Camille was feeling it. It had been years since she willingly called into the office looking for more work to do. Most nights, she ignored the dispatcher altogether and maintained her clearance rates just by stopping the random crimes she spotted on patrol. There was no need to put in extra effort to find trouble in a crime-ridden neighborhood like Pierce. But tonight?

"Seriously, who is this and how did you get B-Girl's call-in ID?" a deep voice responded. Avon King-Corley was in his early thirties and enjoyed the job, especially his nights on dispatch. Everyone knew he spent his work hours checking up on his social media presence between calls, responding to fan emails on his personal phone, and, of course, talking a little bit of shit to the other heroes who protected the same Cargill neighborhoods. Camille was not a fan.

"That's real fucking funny, Avon. Is anything poppin' on the streets or not?" She sounded like her usual self but, honestly, she was in a good mood. Instead of hanging up on the asshole like she usually would have done, she just laughed off the minor disrespect. Plus even she had to admit how rare this call-in was.

"This is the third time tonight that I'm hearing your voice, Baston. You trying to clear out all the crime in Pierce by yourself? Hell of a way to tell us you're retiring."

"Look, dickhead, I don't care if it's the third time or the thirtieth time. Do your job and point me where I need to be." The laughter in her voice was dying fast.

"Well, it's coming on morning rush hour. Good time for officers, bad time for heroes." She heard a tapping noise in the background and knew, just *knew*, that little shit was posting the phrase to his Herogram feed. He thought he was so damn clever. "I just dispatched Stafford and Lawson to break up a big disturbance over at the park. So there's nothing else happening right now and I doubt that's gonna change for the next couple hours at least. You'll probably spend the last hour of your shift just coasting."

"Well, if the park is covered I'm gonna start heading west. If something comes up, call me." She hung up and started a light jog. She had only stopped moving to make the call into dispatch. It was a brief pause, but even through her jumpsuit, Camille's skin had already begun to prickle from the cold. She had been keeping busy all night, partly to stay warm but also due to nervous energy.

For the first time in a long time, Camille saw a light at the end of the tunnel. All those years of grinding for people who didn't appreciate her talents and she finally had a path to advance her own ends while maintaining her status as a veteran hero. The weekend couldn't move quickly enough. It wasn't that she wanted to get back to work, it was that she wanted to get done work and walk back into that coffee shop.

The barista hadn't called. That was a disappointment, but it wasn't a total loss. Camille knew it was jumping the gun when she'd handed her the business card. But since then Camille and Rey had sat down and formulated a plan. Not only could they make enough money to clear their financial woes, they might be able to resurrect B-Girl's long-floundering career in the process. All they had to do was give a better pitch to get the barista on board. They, in this instance, being Camille.

With about an hour to spare, Camille started walking towards the coffee shop where she had parked her SUV. It wouldn't take her that long to get there, but there were ways she could kill time. Case in point—a few blocks from where she started, she noticed a pair of ragged-looking people standing outside a convenience store. They weren't out of place for the neighborhood, but still....

Crime rates naturally dropped a bit once the sun came up. Not everybody who meant to steal at night spotted the right target before morning hit, though, and both were shaking. Camille knew that kind of shake. It wasn't from the cold of the morning. In fact, both appeared to be sweating. They were X-Drah addicts coming down from their latest hits. That made them dangerous.

X-Drah was a designer drug used to mimic some of the effects of Generic Variance Syndrome. Sure, you'd get temporarily heightened physical or mental abilities, but you'd also get increased wear and tear to the eventual, and inevitable, point of permanent damage or death. You couldn't really tell an X-Drah addict that, though. Their mental states were as unstable and unpredictable as their temporary powers, and that made it necessary to take them down.

That fucking drug had kept street-level heroes like her in business for almost ten years.

They positioned themselves on either side of the store's entranceway, perching on the bike racks. It couldn't have been more clear that they had something specific in mind. From where she approached on the other side of the street, Camille could see past band into the plate glass storefront window at their intended victim. She had never been the most diligent of heroes, but she lived for these moments. She could've made the would-be-robbers aware of her presence, but that would've stopped the crime completely. As desperate as they appeared to be, they'd probably just go off and rob someone else.

Instead, Camille calmly walked past them until she was out of their line of sight. Then she crossed over to their side of the street and veered into the alley they'd likely use as a post-theft escape route. Leaning up against the wall and peeking around the corner, she could see one tapping a foot in anticipation. She could see the handle of a switchblade poking out of a pocket, too. They wanted this done quick.

It'll be over quick, alright.

She was stifling a yawn and trying not to think about her morning latte when she heard the convenience store's door chime sound. Turning the corner and walking directly behind the assailants, she watched the crime unfold in full. As soon as the mark was outside of the store, both of them quit their seated positions on the bike racks. The one with the knife raised it to eye level. The other one snatched the mark's purse effortlessly as she raised her hands to protect herself. It was almost balletic.

Camille knew that kind of grace; the purse-snatcher could read physical intentions the way she could. But Camille wasn't about to be intimidated by a drug addict with a watered-down version of her powers. The real threat to that shopper was the one with the knife. She couldn't get a read on what drug-induced powers were at play there. It could be the high had worn off and Camille was looking at someone completely depowered, or she could be looking at someone as strong and fast as Double M. Not terribly likely, but there was really only one way to find out.

"Hey, y'all." As soon as B-Girl spoke up the one with the knife wheeled around to face her, away from the victim.

Perfect.

Camille didn't process; she *reacted*. As he brought the weapon to bear on her with his right hand, she lunged forward and grabbed his wrist with her left. He hadn't even finished spinning towards her before he found himself yanked off-balance directly into her right knee. She was somewhat disappointed not to hear his ribs crack. She was completely unsurprised to hear the clatter of his knife as it hit the ground.

She switched hands and grabbed his now weapon-free arm with her right hand and the back of his neck with her left. It only took a little bit of leverage to guide the criminal face-first into a nearby parked car. Had she taken the time to plan any of this, the delay between thought and deed might've given the other one a chance to strike back or to run away. But Camille's moves required no thought, no planning. They

32

always felt like muscle memory whether she had done them before or not.

When she stood back up straight, the other thief was stiff as a board and still holding the stolen purse. "You wanna hand that back to the lady?" she said, her voice deadly calm. "I don't want you to spill any of her shit while I'm fucking you up."

"I can just sit down," he said as he handed the purse back to its owner. "You don't have to beat me up. I could just sit down on the curb and wait to be arrested."

"Yeah... you could." With that, B-Girl took a swing directly at the thief's nose. He dodged it perfectly. Her next three punches didn't get any closer to landing.

"I'm not doing this! I'm not resisting! I swear. It's the drugs."

This guy had her powers too. In that case, the only way to knock him down in a one-on-one fight was speed and one good shot. Once he was disoriented, she would have the advantage. It was the way she'd lost fights in the past. But right now, as her latte called, that was a lot of effort that she didn't feel like exerting.

"Fine," she said with a sigh. "Sit down and shut up." Without another word, the crook sat down on the sidewalk next to his prone friend. Normally, Camille wouldn't have minded the opportunity to tune him up a bit for slowing down her progress to the coffee shop. But that moment had passed. Plus, she wouldn't do that while witnesses were around. The victim was still standing there, her manicured hands over her mouth.

"Oh my god! Thank you so much for saving me, D-Girl!" The woman approached to shake Camille's hand. Reflexively, Camille returned the handshake, grimaced, and glanced down at the gold monogrammed B on the breast of her dark green uniform. The woman's eyes followed hers. "Oh, I'm so sorry, B-Girl. I'm just a bit rattled by everything. How can I thank you? I can run back inside and get you a cup of coffee or something."

"Nah. No need. I buy from JoMo's on Concord anyway."

"I hear the coffee there is really great. Here, let me at least give you something. Your next cup is on me." She reached into her rescued purse. Camille noticed that she thumbed past several larger bills before pulling out a crisp ten. It would've been a haul for the addicts, that was for sure.

She wasn't supposed to accept gifts, but she was cross about being misnamed, so she pocketed the bill, thanked the woman, and let her walk off. *At least I could close out the day with a win*, she thought as she bent over to pick up the fallen knife. She dialed back in to the office to report her latest catch.

D-Girl? Are you kidding me? Maybe back when I had two husbands. A hint of amusement had just curled her lips when a soft voice answered her call.

"CPD Superhero Dispatch. I'm reading your location, B-Girl."

"Fish? Is that you?" At twenty years young, Marlon Zander was the newest recruit to Cargill's ranks of superpowered heroes. B-Girl hadn't gotten to know them yet beyond the fact that everyone called them Fish.

"At your service. What can I do for you, ma'am?" Strike one.

"First, you can stop calling me 'ma'am.' Where's King-Corley at? He can't be out signing autographs this early, can he?"

34

"There was a big disturbance down at Pierce Park, ma – umm – B-Girl. They needed another hero on site. The Major called me in to work the desk since I'm back part-time now. That gave Avon the green light to go help."

Strike two. Camille knew about Fish breaking a toe while taking down a rogue operator almost a month and a half ago. It wasn't a major injury, but it pulled them off the street for a few weeks and the stop earned them a "Rookie Spotlight" feature in the latest issue of *For Hire*. It had irked Camille when she'd seen it in there on Friday. It irritated her even more this Monday having to hear about it again from this... child. She tightened her grip on the switchblade and began pacing back and forth.

"So instead of just sending me ten blocks over to backup Stafford and Lawson in some real shit, the Major called a kid on crutches off the sidelines to cover for King-Corley while he got sent out here to do my job? Does *that* make sense?"

"I don't make the rules, B-Girl. I just go where they tell me to go." Marlon tried to sound as put out as her. It didn't work.

"Where they tell you to go and whose boots to lick when you get there."

"Okay, that wasn't very nice. Did you only call in to be nasty, or...?"

"While everyone else was focused on what's sounding like the fight of the century, I made a stop on a pair of broke-ass, X'd-out stickup boys. Send me a black-and-white to stuff them in. My shift is over in about twenty minutes and the good mood I started this day with is already gone."

35

"Sorry to hear about your mood, Camille," Marlon said, not sounding the least bit sorry. "Between the trouble at the park and the usually rush hour traffic delays, most of our patrol units are tied up. It might take anywhere between forty-five and sixty minutes before that black-and-white shows up. I'll send them right your way... or maybe I'll forget for a few minutes. I don't know yet. Bye now!" They hung up before Camille could respond.

Strike fucking three.

It was hard enough being passed over by the bosses in favor of grandiose assholes like Avon, but now that fucking twerp Fish was scoring points off her?

Camille was already beyond fed up with her time being wasted, and now who knew how long it would be before the patrol car finally arrived. She stopped pacing and turned back to the crime scene. On the sidewalk, the one assailant was still unconscious. The other was gone without a trace. Her skin prickled again and this time it had nothing to do with the weather. It was going to be a long wait.

Chapter 7

Vanessa

"Why do I put up with this, Van?" JoMo asked as I slid in the door late again.

"Because, MoJo," I said so only he could hear me, getting behind the counter, "I'm the only one who notices that illegal fake tax you put on Corey and Alma's checks and I still haven't told them about it." I tied my apron around my waist. "And because you never noticed that I went on the computers and deleted that illegal fake tax from my own checks about a month after I started here." I raised my voice to normal. "Can I help whoever's next?"

I was feeling myself, and it wasn't just because my makeup was on point. There'd been a super excited little family of Pomeranians out front, my buddy Imani was there to say hi and pick up the latest issue of *For Hire*, and most importantly, the Gizmos had officially made the playoffs. Elise had gotten the message and hadn't contacted me to watch the last game. I had mixed feelings about it, but mostly a sense of relief. The morning rush started slow and Joey used it as an excuse to grumble and stomp his way towards the office, but even that didn't bother me. The day moved fast. There was a short argument about the caloric disparity between two incongruently shaped pieces of pound cake and a clean-up issue with a little kid in the restroom that Joey was only too willing to delegate to me. Other than that, everything kept going at such a rate that I wasn't ready for B-Girl to walk in late for her daily latte. She'd completely slipped my mind.

Her outfit this time was a deep forest green. I wondered how many she owned, and was about to daydream about a closet full of matching uniforms when I realized she was looking right at me.

"JOEY!" she called out, her city accent making the name sound like two separate words.

"Whaddya need, Camille?" Joey rushed the door of his office, wringing his hands and shifting back and forth on his feet. I'd never seen him be so deferential to a customer.

"Cover the counter. This one's on break," she said, pointing at me. She lowered her voice a little but it was no less authoritative. "Make me one of my usuals then come join me at the table."

I jumped to make the latte and almost made a mess of the drink twice. Was B-Girl offended that I hadn't called over the weekend? Was I about to get beaten up for pissing off a superhero? Would a superhero even beat up a civilian and, if so, was there any recourse? I could use the money a lawsuit would bring in.

When the latte was ready, I looked to the seating area to find B-Girl sitting in the far corner facing the counter. I placed the drink on the table and she put away her phone, tilted her head to the empty chair, and said, "Sit."

I almost stumbled hurrying to obey the command and was immediately mad at myself.

B-Girl smiled and warmed her hands on the cup. "What do I call you?"

The hardest question, really. "Van. Ma'am."

"I'mma have enough of you calling me 'ma'am,' thanks. My pronouns are she and her. Yours?" She brought the cup to her lips.

"Same, ma... ummm. Same."

"Camille. My name is Camille or B-Girl or some bastardization of either. I'm not picky. But we already got a problem. See, most people don't wince and look away when giving their names. But you did. So I'll ask you again: what do I call you?"

Well, holy shit. "Vanessa. My name is Vanessa."

B-Girl smiled again. "So you let yourself be called Van—why? To split the difference between what your parents named you and what you would name yourself?"

"Yeah, something like that. No. It's not something like that. It's exactly like that." Most cis people, like my dad, didn't even notice my discomfort. I suddenly liked B-Girl a little more.

"And you fuck up Joey's name sometimes to hide your frustration? You fight the power on some petty shit?"

Did I? Yeah, probably.

"I get it," she said, nodding. "I'm the same way. But don't worry about that with me. I'm going to call you by your name, Vanessa. Or some nickname that doesn't invalidate you, if that's cool with you." She took another leisurely sip of her coffee. "I wanna know more though. What's your story? Why are you here?"

39

"You mean, here in Cargill or here in this coffee shop?"

"Yes," B-Girl said between sips.

I had no idea what to tell this woman, so I just went with the truth. "Well, I'm from here. I grew up here in the city. I went to school here. Outside of a few road trips, I've never really left. I'm working in this shop because I know how to make coffee, I like to eat sometimes, and this place was hiring."

B-Girl laughed at that, like it was roughly the answer she was expecting. "What did you go to school for? What's your passion?"

"Animals, I guess." I blurted out before I could think of a deeper answer.

"You guess? That don't sound like passion." She leaned back and tilted her head.

"I love animals. I do. I went to school for veterinary science. But I never finished."

"Okay... so if you want to be a vet, why are you a barista?"

Sigh. "Because I know how to make coffee, I like to eat sometimes, and this place was hiring."

"I meant, why ain't you finish?"

I paused and sighed again. "I know what you meant. I had something that I lived my life for. But that went away. It's not easy to talk about. After that, I studied to be a vet because I was expected to study *something* and I love dogs. I minored in accounting too since that's what my dad wanted. But those weren't my goals. They weren't even *my* backup plans. When those fell through I just drifted for a while until I landed here."

"No hate, but it looks like you're still drifting. Are your parents helping you?"

"It's just me and my dad," I said. "He and I get along okay and he lets me rent my bedroom for below market value." I smiled to make it sound like a joke. It kind of wasn't though.

"That's good. A job like this could never afford market value. Not if you live anywhere around here." B-Girl took a last deliberate sip of her drink before putting down the cup and pushing it away with her manicured nails. Forest green, of course. "And what's up with that thing you were doing with the numbers on Friday?"

Finally. I'd been waiting for this. It's always about the powers. "It's just a thing I can do."

"Because you're a variant," B-Girl said.

"I am."

"You're a variant who's good with numbers."

"I am."

"And even though you could probably find some desk job and turn that ability into pretty decent money, you won't because the grind you know is preferable to the grind you don't. No pun intended. But regardless of all that, you're tired of this shit, aren't you?"

"I am." Before B-Girl could continue though, I held up my hand. "It's not just that. I was one of the best high school basketball players in the city. I spent thousands of hours in the gym earning that. When the game went away for... reasons, I didn't even get a chance to mourn the loss. I was just expected to switch lanes to something I never worked for and didn't care as much about. It was a lot to process.

41

"I don't love this job, but if it was up to my dad, I'd be working forty hours a week in a cubicle just crunching numbers. A white guy in a bad suit would periodically tell me that I was making an impact on some unseen population, but inside I'd know the truth; I'd only really be helping some shitty company's bottom line." I'd never had to spell out my motivations before. No one ever cared enough to ask. But once I got started, oops, it turned out I had a hard time holding it back. "For someone else, that's fine. I'm not judging. Everybody's gotta eat. But it's not what I want because even if I was doing that, I'd probably still be struggling to get by. Fuck that."

B-Girl's eyes went wide during my rant. I honestly wondered if I had scared her off. But then she spoke again. "Living with your dad doesn't make this easier, does it? He don't understand."

"He doesn't. He's, like, your age." B-Girl raised her eyebrow. I froze for a second, then recovered. "Sorry. I'm so sorry. I just meant that he thinks I'm nothing but a lazy, entitled millennial. I don't want to have to settle for a completely unsatisfying life in order to fight for a marginally less unsatisfying life. Do you know what I mean? It's easier to just do nothing at all."

"I get it. I get it better than you think." B-Girl looked me up and down then leaned back into her chair. "Hearing all this, I gotta apologize for the way I stepped to you before. I thought offering you money would be an easy sell. I didn't realize you were so... principled. Well, let me appeal to those principles.

"I think you and I can do some good work together. We can both use our respective talents to create a positive change in this town, and we can turn our lives around in the process. I wanna offer you an

42

audition: a chance to prove or disprove what I think I know about you. If it works out, we can work together again. If it don't, no hard feelings and we go our separate ways — except for my daily lattes. Either way, we're talking about one night's work, and by the end you'll have enough loot to get a start on a new crib. By this time next week, you can start on some real empowerment—not just screwing up your boss's name. How's that sound?"

I looked at B-Girl in her retro outfit and ridiculous color-coding with her serious, hard eyes and made a snap decision. "It sounds too good to be true. Where do I sign up?"

Chapter 8

Camille

An hour later, this kid, Vanessa, sat in the passenger side of Camille's SUV, now parked up the block from a discount electronics store. Camille had told Joey to work the counter, to pay Vanessa for the rest of her shift, and to consider her missing hours as part of "an enhanced customer service trip." He agreed immediately. What a pushover.

"Why are we watching this electronics store?" Vanessa asked. "Thinking of buying batteries? Because they give away the dead ones free of charge."

Camille wasn't sure if the kid really thought the joke was funny. She raised a hand and pointed at a large black SUV similar to her own pulling up in front of the store. Two young men hopped out of the back seat, each loosely carrying a duffle bag. The taller of the men casually passed his bag back and forth between his hands. The car never shut off as they disappeared into the shop. "Watch and learn, Nessie," Camille said, and the kid sat up straighter.

A few minutes later, two different men stepped outside with their hands tucked inside their jackets. They appeared to be scanning the environment. When they were sure that the coast was clear, the first two men reemerged. This time, they were moving more slowly and struggling under the weight of their now-full duffle bags. They got back in the SUV and were driven away. The scouts retreated inside the electronics store and shut the door behind them.

"Oh my god, this is a stakeout and that shop is a front!" Vanessa's eyes were as big as saucers. "Oh my god! Are we shutting that place down?"

Camille smiled. "You catch on fast." She put the engine in drive and headed off, passing the store as she left. She didn't give it the slightest glance but Vanessa ducked down in her seat a bit. "Word is that the back room is a gambling den. A small one. There's never more than a dozen people playing in there, but they're all whales."

Vanessa turned to Camille and raised an eyebrow. "Whales?"

"High rollers. Big money players. From there, the cash gets put into drugs, guns, and trafficking. If we hit them, there's a lot of dirty money off the streets and one less establishment moving it around."

"Why do you need me though? I can't fight. Wouldn't it make more sense to storm in there with a hundred cops?"

Camille took a breath. "I'm sure you looked me up after I left on Friday. You ain't find a lot of information, did you?"

Vanessa shrugged and looked overly casually out of the window. "I didn't. I was kinda afraid to ask why."

"It's because I never really made my mark on this city, Vanessa," Camille said. The words felt ashy in her mouth. "When I was eighteen,

45

nineteen, New York City recruited me just as hard as Cargill did. My hometown is dead-center between them. I chose Cargill because thirty years ago, it was still on the come-up. Yeah, they're kinda even now, but I wanted to be the face that put this place on the map." She sighed. "It didn't happen. All I really got was an overlooked career and a lot of burned bridges. They don't love B-Girl out here." Camille worked hard to keep her face neutral but the frustration was rising up. There was a reason she didn't talk to people about this. "I know about this place and others like it because I keep my ear to the ground. If I go to my precinct and tell them what's what, they'll give me the run around because they don't like me. By the time they raid the place, the cops on the take will tip off the scumbags running the spot. It'll be empty when we show up and everybody'll blame B-Girl for a bust gone wrong. Nah."

"So what then?"

"I'm gonna smash in there solo. I'm gonna take it down. And I'm gonna take all the credit for the bust... solo."

"Okay. Makes sense. But where do I figure in?"

Camille's face broke into her biggest smile yet. "Criminals aren't economists. They aren't finance majors. The higher-ups, maybe. But the workers are just rough street kids with no place in a real job market. Kinda like JoMo when I sent him up back in the day," she said, to Vanessa's evident shock. "And just like JoMo, they're not great at managing their books. All that extra coffee shop budget you scrounged up to get your boss off your back? You're gonna look at their notes, find the same kind of surplus, and put it in our pockets."

Vanessa's brow furrowed. "That's illegal, though."

46

"You know what's illegal? Everything happening in that back room. You know what's illegal? The fact that I can't go in there like normal police and take that place down legit. If I can't work by the book, I've gotta go off-script."

The kid took a second with her thoughts. "I'm good with all that. What I meant was that *my* involvement was illegal. You're a superhero. You can do whatever you want. But a private citizen walking in there and leaving with any amount of money from a crime scene is illegal."

"A private citizen, yeah. An operator, nah!"

"But I'm not an oper—" Camille started to laugh as Vanessa's mouth dropped open as she started to get it.

Operators were superhuman freelancers. Unlike superheroes, who worked for law enforcement agencies, operators were contractors who could permissibly function outside the constraints of the law. Simply put, they were vigilantes who accepted paychecks.

"Holy shit, are you serious?" Vanessa's voice rose to a near-squeak by the end of the question.

"Yup! As an operator, you can be hired to be on site as long as you don't mess with police business. If something goes wrong, my bosses will check the operator registry to find out that I'm the client and blame me for everything. They'd never blame an innocent kid like you for falling under the spell of a crafty veteran like me. But when everything goes right, all the money on the books, along with any drugs or weapons, would be crime scene evidence subject to search and seizure. Every single dollar those ledgers *miss* would be up for grabs by the operator hired to steal it. With a valid operations contract, law enforcement couldn't even check your bags or pat you down. In that case, no one would ever know I was the client. I'd just be the hero that took down an illegal casino. We'd both be free and clear and the records would be sealed forever."

"And what if the books are well-kept? What if the money we find matches what's on the books perfectly?"

"Then we leave with what we came with, I still get a quality bust, and I'll give you a ride home. I'll even hit a drive-through on the way to pick you up a kid's meal out of my own pocket." Camille laughed, and after a second Vanessa joined in.

The kid then shook her head, looking dazed. Camille couldn't blame her. It was a lot to take in, but overwhelming her wasn't a bad play.

"So when do we do this?" the kid said finally, and Camille knew she had her.

"When the pockets are fattest—Saturday night. If we're good, the whole thing should take less than an hour from the time we walk in to the time the news cameras show up." Camille pulled the car over and put it in park right in front of Vanessa's home.

"You know where I live?" Clumsily, Vanessa pulled off her seatbelt and inched away from the driver's seat.

"You looked me up, I looked you up. No harm, no foul. I'm law enforcement, remember?" Vanessa's body relaxed slightly, which was enough for Camille. "Remember what I said. This can be a game changer for both of us. If you're in, create an operator business profile and text me when you do. Get it done this week and by next Monday your life's gonna look different. It was nice getting to know you today, Vanessa. Now get the fuck out of my car."

Vanessa stumbled out and shut the door behind her. Camille turned the radio on to 99.7 The Beatz and happily swayed with the rhythm as she drove away.

Chapter 9

Vanessa

I got up early the next morning. It'd been forever since I felt this motivated and I wanted to hit the ground running. After a quick shower, I got dressed and headed downstairs to make some food. Breakfast wasn't usually my thing. I typically just filled up on coffee and nibbled snacks from the shop, but today was a new day.

My father was already in the kitchen. I thought he lived there now. He was reading the news on a tablet computer and eating a bowl of cereal when I walked in.

"Hey, Dad!"

"Good morning, Van." He glanced at his watch. "Getting an early start."

"Yeah, I am." I pulled eggs, cheese, and a loaf of bread out of the fridge. "I was given a chance to do a little freelance work last night after I left JoMo's. I wanted to get up early and fill out the job application." I kept it as close to the truth as I could without giving away too much. I didn't know how my dad would feel about me working as an operator. Operators had a reputation for either getting into danger or being the danger. I doubted he'd be comfortable with either possibility.

"A job application for a freelance gig that was already offered to you? What kind of work is this?" Dad put the spoon down and turned his chair to look at me. He was suspicious. If he took off his glasses, the jig was up. I had to play it smooth.

"I think they're just trying to establish a line of paperwork. Y'know, in case we want to continue working together after the first project wraps up." Not a drop of sweat. Ice water in my veins. No lies told. I cracked a pair of eggs into a bowl and began beating them with a fork.

"I guess that makes sense. So, you're leaving the coffee shop then?" He smiled and raised an eyebrow. I think he thought it was funny somehow. The eyebrow thing, not me leaving the coffee shop.

But damn, I hadn't even started my freelance job and he wanted to fast forward to my better tomorrow. I guessed I should be happy that he thought I could even *have* a better tomorrow but I held back a sigh. Being careful not to spill any of the freshly beaten eggs, I put the bowl in the microwave, set the timer, and put two slices of bread in the toaster before turning back to him.

"Not yet. I'd really need to see where this goes first. It seems like it'll pay well, but if isn't a steady paycheck I don't want to burn any bridges. I'm just gonna do this in my spare time."

"That's very responsible of you," Dad said, now fully engaged. He hadn't even noticed that his tablet powered down and he wasn't holding the spoon at all anymore. Glasses remained in place. "What kind of business is this, anyway? What sort of work will you be doing?"

"It's sort of an independent startup." The misleading truths were flowing smoothly now as I peeled a slice of cheese off the stack and returned all the food to the fridge. "It's a kind of financial management biz that moves capital around to fund community initiatives. I'm coming on as a consultant to monitor for and redirect any budget surpluses." I'd like to thank the Academy. Honestly, while my acting definitely earned some kind of merit, being able to see my dad without his usual frown of disappointment was its own reward. Vanessa Copeland: Daughter of the Year.

"Wow, Van! That sounds like a big deal. Nothing my kid can't handle though. I'm really proud to see how motivated you are to do something important. I know I've been kinda hard on you, but it's only because I see so much potential in you. I just don't want to see it wasted."

Trying to let the words slide off me, I took the bread from the toaster and made a sandwich with the slice of cheese and the now-cooked egg. Nice. "Yeah, Dad. I know. I just really needed the right opportunity. Thanks for being patient with me." I took a second to hug him then grabbed my sandwich. I told you I was a fantastic daughter.

I turned, stuffed my face full of delicious egg and cheese, and headed back up the stairs to my room. The laptop and web browser were already open. Using my sandwich-free hand, I entered the address for the Extralegal Operation Registry. It was a government-run website, which was intimidating. The homepage consisted of muted colors, a constantly updated news feed, and a list of *For Hire*'s operator power rankings. I didn't recognize any of the names on it, but it's not like I ever really read *For Hire* and operators weren't known for being household names. Skipping past all that, I put the mouse cursor over a tab that read "Operator Resources" and clicked the drop-down menu's first link, "Create An Account."

The application process was almost identical to signing up for a credit card or filling out tax forms or applying for any other job. Since retail therapy was one of my chief forms of self-care, my contact information was completed automatically by my browser. Sweet! The unfamiliar fields were related to my powers.

The form allowed you to select Non-Powered, Self-Powered, GVS/Variant, Other, and Decline to Answer. Curious, I tried each in turn. Most of them opened a text box requesting further details, except for Decline to Answer, which required reasons. Once I settled on GVS/Variant, new checkboxes appeared to report each ability. I quickly scanned through the names for powers both familiar and unfamiliar. They listed Enhanced Speed, Enhanced Strength, Enhanced Perception (Spatial), Enhanced Perception (Language), Enhanced Perception (Physical). I even spotted B-Girl's ability, Body Control. I chose the one that felt best suited to what I can do: Pattern Recognition.

The next page had me enter my financial information and bank accounts, state and federal tax forms, and submit to credit and background checks, among other things. After that was the documentation for medical status and insurance liability. The disclaimers were pretty damn detailed. They covered every eventuality. I guessed they had to. Years of filling out online forms got me accustomed to just scrolling straight past these and submitting the form. This time I slowed down long enough to at least skim each section. It didn't change the eventual outcome but the added diligence made me feel safer and more confident. I finally clicked "OK" at the bottom of the page and was now officially an operator. At least, I would be in one to three business days once my application was reviewed and approved.

Vanessa Copeland: *Operator?*

Chapter 10

Camille

After finishing a bit of work that included a draft for Vanessa's first contract, Camille closed her laptop and pulled out her phone. She preferred typing on a real keyboard, but she used the phone for almost everything else as it allowed her to be in motion. It wasn't like she would trip or walk into something, not with her power. She opened her banking app as she headed downstairs and scanned the account balances. She knew what she'd find there, but with the job coming up, she wanted to give herself some additional motivation.

In the basement, she could hear the familiar sounds of her husband moving around, along with some unfamiliar rustling that had her tilting her head.

"Things are getting moving, Rey," she said as she opened the door and descended the stairs. "I just made an operator client profile and Number Girl hit me with her account details. All we gotta do is finish the job listing and send it—um—what is this?" Rey sat on the basement floor surrounded by sheets of grid paper, tiny figurines, and multiple sets of dice.

"It's a C&C set, babe." He turned and looked at all the items placed around him, grinning with palpable enthusiasm.

"And what the fuck is a C&C set?"

His face dropped.

"Creatures and Catacombs? It's a tabletop roleplaying game. Been around since the 1970s. I'm surprised you haven't at least heard about it."

"Okay, I've *heard* of Creatures and Catacombs. Never as C&C though, and I damn sure ain't know what it looked like." She put her hand to her head and gave herself a second to think. "I guess what I'm asking is, why's it here? Is now the moment to be taking on new hobbies?"

"It's an old hobby, baby. I used to play all through junior high and high school. I didn't buy anything! I found all this stuff in a box. Actually," he said, drawing the word out, "I gave it up when I met you."

"And why'd you do that?"

"C&C is really nerdy. I met this pretty girl and wanted her to think I was cool." He waggled his eyebrows.

Camille burst out in a giggle. How long had it been since that had happened? "Oh, I see how it is. Now that we're married for a couple of decades, you can come out the closet with this geek shit? You think you don't gotta impress me no more?" She couldn't stop her smile.

He looked back down at the papers. "I'm not playing it. I'm using the dungeon mat and the character tokens to help plan the operation."

"You're helping to plan the operation?" She couldn't keep the incredulity out of her voice.

He looked a little hurt. "Why the surprise?"

"You've never had an opinion, let alone an entire plan, having to do with my work in the field."

"Well," he said, sitting up straight, "not only do I have a plan, I got a blueprint." Rey reached behind him and grabbed a mailing tube. From it, he produced a roll of paper which he laid flat in front of him. "It's the layout of the electronic store where your casino is *and* each update they got a permit for."

Color her impressed. "Where did you get that from?"

"The county permit agency. Whatever that building is about now, its construction was all up to code and that makes it part of public record. I was talking to a couple of friends in construction and the idea came to me."

"Wow! This is really helpful, baby. But since when do you have friends in construction?"

"Since I started... um...."

"Since you started what?" Her eyes narrowed.

"Look, don't get mad, but I started working a side job at one of the Quinn sites. The foreman is someone I knew from back in the day. He knows we're struggling with cash, so he offered to pay me under the table for about twenty hours a week of manual labor."

"When the hell do you have twenty free hours?"

"It's just a few hours here and there while you're asleep after your shift." He shifted his weight around a little. Camille steeled herself; whatever he said next was going to upset her even more. It was his tell he'd been hiding something. "For the last, uh, six months."

She let out a breath. "I noticed you been looking busy. Tired. And here I was waiting for you to introduce me to some new boo, when really you're sneaking out to hide money from me?"

"I'm not hiding money." He finally got to his feet to look his wife in the eyes.

"Where's it at then?" She made a show of looking around as if expecting to spot a bag overflowing with loose cash behind the water heater.

"It's in the fridge and in your gas tank and in the new pipes under the sink. It ain't much more than walking-around money, babe, but I use most of it to cover household expenses. Y'know, so I don't have to go dipping into the joint account."

She ran her hands over her head. "You could've told me. You should have."

"You don't always like when things change, babe. I just wanted to do a bit more. Being your manager doesn't always fill my hours and I felt like I could help out in other ways. You mad?" He took a tentative step toward her.

"No," she said in a tone that suggested otherwise. But she closed the gap and put her arms around him. "But all that is dead. If this job goes well, it could cover us financially for a while."

"That depends on the kid, right? How are you gonna pay her?"

"I'm taking all the real risks, so she can just get ten percent of whatever we take out of there. She's a teenager living at home with a single parent. She'll be happy with whatever she gets."

"Sounds good. Let's talk about this plan, then, since my baby is taking all the risks."

"Okay... but don't ever hide anything from me again." He was right. She didn't like change—except when she was in control of it.

"Including that new boo you mentioned? I mean, I'm a big man with a healthy appetite." He waggled his eyebrows again, trying for another laugh.

She covered her mouth so he couldn't see the smile. "You better stop, Reynolds."

His hands started wandering, and the sigh she let out was a happy one for once.

Chapter 11

Vanessa

The rest of the work week passed like molasses through a sieve. I couldn't keep my mind off my first extralegal operation, but each part of the process felt like a slog. The wait for my application's approval, the wait for B-Girl to send me the contract offer, then the wait for the day of the operation itself, all of it broken up by eight-plus-hour days of slinging coffee. Even my daily B-Girl sighting couldn't break up the monotony. She had resumed her custom of all but ignoring me. Fun.

But tonight was the night. I took a cab to the address B-Girl gave me, which turned out to be a house in Cargill's Foster Heights area. This was the nice side of town. The lawns were well-tended and the cars in the driveways were expensive.

I'd heard about the real estate strategy of buying the worst house on the best block. I wondered if B-Girl was familiar with it as well. Her place was clearly the least of the neighborhood's residences. Aside from being one of the smallest, the other nearby homes appeared to have recent upkeep, additions, and renovations. The one I stood in front of... did not. I jogged up the stairs on the side of the house's single-car driveway and rang the bell.

When the door opened, a large black man stood framed in the doorway. This guy was really tall—maybe six feet, three inches. He was broad too. I couldn't have squeezed past him if I wanted to. He took a moment to size me up before finally speaking.

"You're the numbers chick, huh?"

"I guess I am. And you must be the complete stranger guy." I leaned back until I had to step down a bit. Taking in how huge he was required a bit of additional perspective.

Maybe he started slouching, but he seemed to shrink a little as he leaned forward to offer his hand. "Reynolds Sterling-Baston. Everyone calls me Rey, though."

"Vanessa Copeland. Everyone calls me—you know what? Vanessa's fine." I shook his hand and he backed up to allow me to enter.

"Nice to meet you, Vanessa. Camille's getting ready. I'll bring you up to the loft." He started towards a stairway and I followed closely behind him.

Moving through B-Girl's home was eye-opening. The interior was in stark contrast to the exterior, borderline gaudy with modern conveniences. The appliances in the kitchen were all top-of-the-line. Big screen televisions were in every room I passed and each had several devices connected, including home theater components, game consoles, and media players. The walls were bare, but I could see faded halos around slightly brighter paint that indicated that they hadn't always been so empty.

The only area of the house that seemed to have an adorned wall was the loft. "Wait right here," Rey said as he left the room through a far doorway.

Even if he hadn't been leading me to this room, I'd have paused to take in the wall full of framed photos. It appeared to be a retrospective on B-Girl's career. There were lots of images taken with colleagues, but almost no action shots or pictures near any crime scenes. I wondered if that was because she didn't have many noteworthy stops in her career or if it was just bad taste to take personal photos on the job.

With the amount of colorful outfits on display, I could tell that most of these were photos of B-Girl with other heroes. I didn't recognize any of the faces save one. In one framed picture, the country's most popular hero stood tall with an arm around a grimacing Camille. I leaned forward to get a better look when I heard light footsteps behind me. "So you know Double M?" I asked, trying not to sound too eager.

"Of course I know her. We're both superheroes in the same city. She's my goddamn captain." B-Girl strolled into the room dressed in her usual jumpsuit, this time in a red so deep it could pass for maroon in certain light.

"How is she in person?" I finally stopped staring at the picture and turned to face my host. Given the snappish tone in her voice, maybe this wasn't the line of questioning I should've been following, but counterpoint: Double M was hot.

Just then, Rey leaned into the room and held up a black leather belt that held a pair of holsters, each of which contained a long black knife. Camille looked at the belt, thought for a moment, and said, "It's a big night for us. This is gonna be on the news. It's less complicated with no bodies."

Wordlessly, Rey nodded and left the room. B-Girl fixed me with her attention again. "You see that Shae Livingston interview the other day? The one where Double M talked about oldheads giving her a hard time?"

"I was nodding off to sleep by that point, but I remember her saying something like it. Was that about you?"

B-Girl sighed loudly and took a seat on the couch. "It wasn't *just* about me. But yeah."

"Was she being mean? She seems so nice." I slipped off my backpack and took a seat across from her.

"She *is* nice. Too nice. She blew into town all full of smiles and colorful hair and talking about honor and duty. It was the kind of idealism that either inspires you or exhausts you. Her real crime though, as far as we were concerned, was that she showed us all up. She didn't even know all the street names on her first beat before she cleaned up that entire neighborhood damn near single-handedly. She became a media darling when she should've just been a rookie bringing us coffee. There was a feeling among a lot of us vets that she jumped the line."

That sounded familiar. When I made the high school team, the older players didn't like the idea that a punk-ass freshman like me took the starting job away from a beloved graduating senior. I got bullied during the training camps and pre-season. That changed once we started winning real games. After that, the hate got redirected from me and toward anyone who wasn't supporting me.

"I can see how that might make people resent her," I said. Vanessa Copeland: Diplomat. "But then why do you have the picture?"

Before she could answer, Rey leaned back into the room and held up a satchel; it appeared to hold a half dozen thick metal rods. B-Girl shook her head.

"There's not gonna be that many guards back there. Plus, we making statements tonight, baby." She turned back to me and Rey disappeared for a second time.

"Because as insufferable as M is, she's the real deal. I've made a career out of pissing people off and she's never let me rattle her. Not once. I called that bitch a 'stupid purple cunt' to her face. Y'know what she did not sixty seconds after that?"

"No. What?" I asked. I found myself scooting to the edge of my seat. I may not have been much into superheroes and I might've only asked about Double M because I hoped she was into sporty baristas, but drama was drama and I was here for it.

"That fucking do-gooder made me a better hero," B-Girl said, rolling her eyes.

I blinked. Not the answer I was expecting. "How'd she do that?"

"She told me that she studied my training footage and fight data and designed a series of magnets—fucking magnets!—that could make me a more effective fighter."

"Magnets? I don't get it. And no offense, but I can't see you just accepting her help like that."

"At first I didn't. I told her right where she could stick those magnets. Then she noticed that some of my uniforms were damaged and stitched up. The endorsement deal that kept me geared up had already expired. So, M buys me a dozen new outfits with the works." She stood up, did a smooth turn, and gestured to her current jumpsuit. "We're talking stab-resistant fibers, kevlar plating, a whole rainbow of colors, they still look as fly as my old gear, and she had her fucking magnet tech already built in. She called it a birthday present and made a big deal out of it in the squad room where everyone could see. She basically embarrassed me into accepting a dope gift."

"I hate to say it, but that's actually pretty sneaky-awesome."

Camille scrunched up her face. "She's the only one who could get away with that crap. I still don't really like her. But it made me respect her. It takes a lot of heart to play the game the way she plays it."

For the third time, Rey entered the room. This time he was holding an aluminum bat and what appeared to be a studded metal baseball. B-Girl nodded approvingly.

"That's what I'm talking about. Go start the car and we'll be right down." With that, Rey left again.

"Is he your sidekick or something?" I asked.

"He's my husband. You're my sidekick," she responded. "Speaking of which, when you made your operator profile you named yourself 'V-Girl'?" There was amusement in her voice.

Shit! I forgot about that. With two hands, I pulled the collar of my hoodie up almost over my mouth.

"I didn't know what to put as my codename and I was too excited to spend more time thinking about it. So I just dropped in the first thing I could think of. I can change it."

"You're gonna have to." Camille laughed as she held out a hand to help me out of my seat. "Nothing's going wrong tonight, but if something did, the records would get unsealed. It can't look like we went into this together."

She was right. I'd have to think on it and pick a more appropriate name. That was Future-Vanessa's problem though. In that moment, my focus had to be my first spin as an operator.

B-Girl led me outside to where her SUV was parked. Rey already had the engine running, the GPS set, and the radio tuned to The Beatz. It was time.

Chapter 12

Camille

Rey parked the SUV half a block away from the location of the night's adventure. They were in the same spot that Camille had taken Vanessa for their stakeout earlier in the week.

"An unexpected SUV with tinted windows pulling up right out front will raise alarms, so we're just gonna walk up the street like random pedestrians and Rey's gonna stay here until we're inside." She reached into the front seat and tapped her husband on the shoulder. He responded by passing back the metal bat and ball he showed her back at the house.

"When do I go inside?" Camille could see the moisture on Vanessa's hands as they opened and closed around the strap of the empty duffle bag she was holding. That adrenaline, hopefully, would keep the kid alert.

Camille shook her head and her long braided ponytail floated over her right shoulder, landing perfectly in her hands. She loved the routine of weaponizing her body and she moved as slowly and deliberately as time allowed so she could savor it.

"You're gonna be following me in. Close but not too close. I'm in the mix. You're in the cut. I want to be able to see you but not feel you. Ya feel me?"

Vanessa nodded, and Camille threaded a metal post through the end of her ponytail, then secured it in place with a thick hair tie. Next, she screwed the studded ball to the end of that post, creating a mace. Out of the pockets of her faux velour jumpsuit, she pulled out a pair of gloves. The gloves were, of course, the same shade of red as the rest of the outfit with the exception of black carbon fiber reinforcements at each knuckle. As she slipped them on, she noticed the younger woman staring at her with eyes wide. The attention made her smirk as she grabbed the bat and opened the car door.

"Pick your jaw up off the floor and let's move."

Camille set a steady but casual pace up the block—not so fast as to raise attention, but not slow enough to appear to be creeping up. The baseball bat was tucked under the superhero's arm almost blatantly in plain sight. Glancing over her shoulder, she spotted Vanessa staring at her back, eyes swaying back and forth, hypnotized by the swinging mace in her ponytail. Camille enjoyed the kid's wide-eyed enthusiasm. She'd forgotten what it felt like to be that young and innocent. All she remembered was how to do this. Turning in a sharp arc, Camille entered the electronics shop.

The small business was claustrophobic, with rows of stereo systems, the left wall full of oversize televisions and the right with cellphone accessories. The glass case near the sales terminal was tightly arrayed with mobile devices. Packed into this tiny space were three other humans—armed guards.

The first two were talking near the front of the store. The last one was near the back door and, she noticed, left-handed. Before any of them could take in the new arrival, she launched her baseball bat like a javelin between the closest pair. Lunging forward, she simultaneously swung the heavy ponytail mace into the nose of the gunman to her right while squaring up against the one to her left.

Mace to ya face, she thought to herself as her body took over. One guard dropped as the second got served a three-punch combination. In the distance, a crunch and a cry of pain signaled that the thrown bat had landed perfectly on target: the third man's left hand. Grabbing the closest guard with both hands, Camille spun and used the momentum to slam him into his fallen friend. Both were out of the game.

She took a second to disarm each man and disable their weapons completely. Then she casually strolled to the back to find the final guard attempting, with his undamaged right hand, to reach the weapon holstered just below his right arm. It wasn't going well.

One more combination of punches and he was out too. Once the last guard's firearm was out of commission, Camille took its owner by the hand and dragged him over to the door of the back room. She slapped his palm onto a touchpad embedded on the wall. The pad glowed green in response and the door slid open. The sound of another door opening and closing drew her attention back to the front.

She watched Vanessa cautiously enter the store. Either the guards went down even faster than she thought or else Vanessa was hesitant to get her first taste of real danger.

Camille took a bit of pride at the shock on Vanessa's face as she saw the unconscious men that had been left up front.

"Lock that door behind you and catch up, Ness." She didn't wait for a response. She picked up her baseball bat and headed through the door. From behind her came the locking of a deadbolt and the awkward steps of Vanessa trying to navigate around several prone bodies and dismantled gun parts.

Multiple drive-bys had told Camille everything she needed to know about the first floor, but now she was going purely on Rey's plans and some guesswork. The stairs in front of her should lead to the converted basement where the casino resided, where there was no telling what to expect beyond an assumed headcount of guards and players based on the size of the space. It was only a matter of time before the casino crew tried to communicate with the front door team. She needed to move quickly to maintain the element of surprise.

She crept down the stairs and the sound of jumbled voices grew louder with each step. Vanessa shut the door silently, leaving the basement's muted red glow as the only light on the staircase. Once her eyes adjusted, Camille had just enough visibility to locate the source of the glow—the casino. The whole area was blocked off by a thick curtain but the sound of a roulette table was clear from within.

"By my count, there should be about five more guards, a couple of workers, and maybe a dozen players," Camille whispered as she sensed Vanessa closing in behind her. "The workers and the players we don't gotta worry about, they're unarmed and probably passive. We're catching them with their pants down. The guards are a problem. They'll all have guns and the advantage of knowing the layout better than we do."

"So what do we do?" Vanessa asked, her voice barely audible.

"We do the same shit we just did." Camille tossed her head back and forth. Her armed ponytail, which had been draped over her shoulder resting lightly on her chest, coiled into a tight bun on the crown of her head. The glow illuminated Vanessa's incredulous expression and Camille had to stop herself from laughing.

Vanessa blinked and shook her head. "What same shit, exactly? By the time I got inside the building, everyone was down."

"Okay, then I'll do the same shit I just did. You'll just have to stick closer if you want to watch this time. We gotta go right now before any of these guys tries to call upstairs. Be careful in there." With that, Camille stormed through the only visible break in the curtains. Vanessa was close—but not too close—on her heels.

The casino, if you could call it that, was just the open area between the curtained partition and a back wall with a single door. The layout contained a pair of blackjack tables, a roulette wheel, and a large poker table. Each station had a dealer and a few players currently engaged. They all froze as Camille grabbed the first guard she could see and pushed him from his station straight into the center of the room.

There was no wasted motion as Camille let go of the guard and knocked him out with a backhand swing from the bat. In the middle of her follow through, she shoved the heel of the aluminum bat with her free hand. It flew like a spear straight at a second guard on the room's far right. Like it did to the back door guard upstairs, the bat's end cap made solid contact with flesh—this time, the guard's forehead. He was laid flat.

Meanwhile, Camille dove to the far left where another guard waited. This third one was the sharpest of the group as he already had his knife out. A gun would've cleared the distance better, but would of course also be a threat to the casino's high profile clientele.

Despite obvious martial arts skill, the guard couldn't touch Camille. Her body moved as if she were psychic, never anywhere he needed her to be. Every slash was met with a lazy expression and a dangerously-near miss, blatantly toying with him. One pirouette later and Camille's tight bun unraveled and smashed its ponytail-mace directly into the knife-wielding guard's temple.

Less than twenty seconds had passed and three of the four visible guards were already knocked out. The fourth just trembled, his hands hovered over his gun belt as if afraid to touch it. These weren't really trained professionals. They were just men with weapons, which was never going to be the same thing. Camille walked calmly over to him.

"What's the name of the guy in the vault?" The guard didn't respond. His mouth hung open and his fingers twitched.

Camille opened her hand and drew closer. "The guy in the vault. Tell me his name, *now*!"

When she got within punching range and cocked her arm behind her, the guard cracked. "Teddy. His name is Teddy."

"Thank you," Camille said while flexing her fingers and turning into a second spin. After flying through the players at the roulette wheel, she retrieved the aluminum bat just in time to swing it into the guard's face.

"*Teddy!*" she called through the door on the casino's far wall. "I know you probably got your gun out in there, buddy. But I'm a superhero and I've got an operator out here with me. Either you surrender to me or I'm sending her in there with you. Your choice." Glancing back at Vanessa, Camille threw her a smirk and a wink.

Vanessa was, of course, no danger to the vault guy, but the threat of an operator was enough that he opened the door and tossed out his weapon. Camille immediately knocked him out like the other staff. The rest of the room was motionless, eyeing Vanessa as if *she'd* been the one to take down five men. Camille felt offended on behalf of all superheroes.

"You're up, kid." Camille hiked a thumb at the now-open vault door. She hefted her bat over her shoulder and began strolling among the tables.

Chapter 13

Vanessa

It'd been less than five minutes since B-Girl and I walked in from the street and I had already lost count of how many unconscious men I'd stepped over. At least now I knew what body control was. It sure wasn't dancing. Mostly.

I walked past B-Girl through the vault door and closed it behind me. I heard Camille shout something at the casino's patrons, but it didn't register. She was controlling the crowd and I... I was doing this.

Inside there was a single desk and two massive shelving units. I knew we were in a hurry but I couldn't help but take a quick lap of the room. On the shelves to my left were stacks of cash separated by denomination. On the right were huge taped packages that I could only assume contained drugs. I couldn't identify what kinds, but this was how they looked in the movies. Shit! I was *in* a movie. This must be what it felt like.

I shook off the thought and went back to the task. The desk was where I needed to be. On it sat a calculator, a money counter, an open ledger, and a laptop computer docked to a pair of large monitors —

everything you'd need to do some quickie accounting. Well, not everything. You'd also need diligence. It seemed as if Teddy had let his focus lapse. Layered over the spreadsheet application on the computer was a browser window streaming music videos.

I sat my empty duffle bag on the desk and saddled up to the terminal. The open spreadsheet appeared to be a shared document containing several tabs labeled by address. The active tab matched their current location—the casino's financial records. A quick scan showed that the count was taken every hour on the hour. Cash was picked up every three hours. We'd arrived about forty minutes after the last one. This was going to be easy. What B-Girl could do with her body and armed assailants, I could do with my eyes and that data. Kinda sorta.

I meant to only flip through the last few pages in the ledger, but I ended up sweeping through all forty-seven handwritten pages, pausing to note dates, addresses, and especially figures. After doing another inspection on about a week's worth of numbers, I compared them to the spreadsheet and found what I needed. I just had to be sure. Taking a slower lap around the room, I re-examined the labels on the drug packages and the neatly organized cash stacks. I walked to the vault door and whistled for B-Girl to come over. She was casually picking up and dismantling the weapons of the fallen guards. Everyone else was huddled together sitting on the floor along the right wall.

"What's up?" B-Girl asked, dropping her voice as she strolled over. The crowd was still and silent. No one wanted to take a chance at incurring her wrath.

I lowered my voice too. "It's done. Well, almost done. I just wanted to run it past you before finishing up."

"Already? It hasn't even been ten minutes."

"Yeah, and that's with a double- and triple-check of all the numbers. Let me tell you what I found." B-Girl turned her gaze back towards the casino floor and leaned on the wall next to the door as I continued. "It's like you said, this place is a storeroom for drugs and drug money. That stuff is well documented. What's poorly documented is the take from the casino itself. The players on the floor now? Their losses over the last four or five hours are mostly unaccounted for. To the tune of two hundred thousand dollars."

"That much in four hours?"

"It looks like it's been tallied wrong for the last eight hours. But the bulk of that is from the last four or five, yeah."

"So what do you need to do now?"

"I just need to grab and go. Twenty stacks of hundreds should do it."

"You can't live your life only spending Benjis, girl. Swap in at least twenty K in twenties."

I nodded and went back into the vault, closing the door behind me. Opening the duffle bag, I threw in twenty-eight banded sets of bills. When I was finished, I looked down inside the bag. There was so much *space*. Years of watching heist movies had filled me with visions of hefty containers swelling with loose cash. Instead, there I was with enough money to change my life and it all weighed less than ten pounds total. I could've fit it all in an oversized purse.

When I stepped back out, B-Girl was on her phone. "Yeah, the electronics store at 20th and Harrison. If you want the exclusive, you need to get your cameras here fast. This is a huge bust. Don't get scooped." She put away her phone and looked at me. "If you're done, head to the car and be out. We'll settle up after. I'm gonna wait here for the media to show. These folks are about to have a bad day."

With one last hopefully-professional looking nod, I started to walk out of the casino and suddenly stopped. I hadn't looked at any of the gamblers on my way in, since everything had happened so fast, but now a familiar face caught my eye. I made my last quick call of the night. "Hey, B! She leaves with me." I hoped I sounded confident while pointing at a tall woman near the poker table.

B-Girl's lips pursed. "What? Why? You know her?"

"Yeah," I said, "It's *Dawn Taylor.*"

B-Girl shrugged.

"*Break-of-Dawn* Taylor? Star point guard for the Cargill Gizmos?'

B-Girl shrugged again.

"Look, the playoffs are about to start," I told her. "We need her on the court. For the good of the city!"

Just then a middle-aged man stood up next to where Dawn Taylor was seated. "I run a financial institution that employs thousands of Cargill residents. If anybody here represents the good of the city, it's me."

What an asshole. It wasn't even what he was saying that ticked me off. It was the entitlement he said it with. You could tell this guy was used to preferential treatment. You know who wasn't used to preferential treatment?

"Those Cargill residents you employ, sir. What's the minimum wage for your employees?" I called out loudly as I walked over to where he stood.

"I, uh, I don't know. I'd have to call my—" Without even thinking, I shut the man up with a single swing. It was the first time I'd punched anyone since my sophomore year of high school. And though my hand and wrist probably hurt more than that jerk's face did, we were both equally surprised by the impact. Behind me, I heard B-Girl start to laugh.

"You heard the lady, Taylor. Get up and get the fuck out of here."

I gave one last nod to B-Girl in thanks, gripped my bag tightly, and headed through the curtain. Dawn Taylor was following close behind me. Dawn Taylor!

"You're a fan of the Gizmos, huh?" She sounded half-amused and half-nervous as we walked along.

"Yeah. Lifelong. But more importantly, I'm a fan of *you*. I've been following your career since college. I even modeled my jump shot after yours." Okay, I was going for it. "You're kind of my hero."

"Thanks! You're pretty tall. Do you still play?"

"Not really. Not since high school. Back then I won back-to-back city championships and even went all-state." Ugh, this part of the conversation. I could feel my body tense up.

"Get out of here! If you're that good, why aren't you still at it? You look young enough to still be on a college scholarship somewhere."

If anyone would understand, it would be Dawn Taylor, but I still couldn't bring myself to say it. "It's kind of a long story."

I could feel her eyes on me. Finally, she said, "I didn't mean to press. I appreciate the support though. I've got nothing but love for my fans. Do I owe you anything for this?"

A laugh burst out of me. Imagine Dawn Taylor owing me anything. I unlocked the shop's front door and turned to her before pushing it open.

"Yeah. Get us out of the first round this year. And stop gambling in shady-ass drug spots."

She nodded and left the building. I gave my team's star player a last look as she walked down the street. She had her phone out now. No doubt she was calling a car to come collect her. My ride was already waiting. I headed in the opposite direction and hopped back into B-Girl's SUV after checking to make sure I hadn't been followed.

"You could've gotten in the front," Rey said from the driver's seat. He was listening to sports talk radio. The on-air personalities were talking about the hockey playoffs which had just begun.

"I didn't want to take B-Girl's seat for the ride back," I said with a shrug. Fact is, I didn't enjoy being that close to Rey. Something about him set me on edge. Not "imminent danger" on edge. Just "don't get too comfortable" on edge.

"Nah. Camille has to stay and deal with the media. I'm bringing you home now before the cameras arrive. I'll swing back around later to pick up my girl." He put the car in drive and headed past the place I just left. "How was the job? What was the take?"

"Total we pulled in two hundred thou."

He whistled. "And you're getting what? Ten percent? At nineteen years old, that's a good haul. Enough for you to buy yourself something nice."

"I'm twenty-two." Rey didn't respond and I didn't care. He was right. Getting my own place and maybe finishing school would be a lot easier than it was a half hour before.

The drive back to my home was swift and mercifully quiet as I replayed the night in my head. The job took no time and, with B-Girl, I was never in any danger. I felt good. Well, I was shaky as I came down from the adrenaline rush, but all in all, I thought it had gone well. Not that I had anything to compare it to.

As we approached my house, I reached into the duffel bag and removed five stacks of twenties and one stack of hundreds and put them in my backpack. Twenty thousand dollars. Less than two pounds of added weight, but still enough to change the trajectory of my life. When Rey pulled up in front of my house, I thanked him politely. He gave me a fatherly smile and said, "Good work."

Maybe I'll quit my job tomorrow, I thought as I strolled up to my front door.

Chapter 14

Camille

"Good morning. My name is Major Anthony J. Morella." The media room was charged. The gathered reporters were here all the time, but rarely for such a big deal. Camille stood on the dais next to her direct superior, Double M. Both were behind the man speaking at the podium, just over his left shoulder.

"Last night, April 8th at around 11 p.m., the Cargill Police Department infiltrated an illegal underground gambling operation being run from the basement of an electronics store. This casino, which was frequented at the time by several influential business and political figures, also doubled as a stash house for an as-of-yet unidentified organized crime enterprise. Found on the scene were several armed guards, over two million dollars in cash, and just under an estimated half a million dollars in illegal drugs.

"The takedown of this establishment was led by veteran superhero B-Girl." The major paused for a moment to acknowledge the day's hero. Camille had to squint and turn her head away from the flashbulbs. She could barely hear herself think over the sound of cameras clicking. This was her moment. Or was it? "But this couldn't have been done without the stellar investigative work of the entire Cargill Police Department. In the coming days, we'll be working with detectives and leaning on all of the casino's employees to identify which crime syndicate this all belongs to. The district attorney's office is chomping at the bit to either put away all of those employees or to trade up for their superiors. There's a major player out there having a really bad morning and we mean to comfort them with a cozy pair of handcuffs and a nice warm jail cell.

"The CPD kicked butt last night and I couldn't be prouder or more excited about what we're going to turn this bust into. I've got to go, but I'm gonna let the media officer handle any questions about last night's operation. Thank you."

A thin man in a white shirt and dress slacks stepped onto the dais and over to the microphone. Double M led the way through a door just off the speaker's platform. Once they were clear of the stage, Morella rounded on Camille.

"*Baston*! My office. Now!" The major's volume jolted the officers tasked with transporting last night's haul to the evidence lockers. The journalists would've heard the order through the walls if they weren't all shouting questions at the media rep.

Double M patted Camille on the shoulder and walked towards her office without a word. Camille looked at her retreating back with disgust. Some support she got there!

The major headed in the opposite direction and Camille followed, growing more antsy and annoyed with each step. When she entered his office after him, she shut the door and quickly popped down into a chair before he could invite—or order—her to sit.

"What's your problem, Morella?"

The major pulled out his chair but didn't sit. Instead, he stared down at her with an expression not unlike the one she'd given Double M.

"My problem is that we have a procedure in this precinct. You don't just stroll into a bust by yourself. You report in. You call for backup. You notify your superior officer. *You get a goddamn warrant!* We've got millions in cash and narcotics and we don't even know who any of it belongs to."

"By the time I did any of that, that casino and those players would've been long gone. Besides, I didn't need a warrant. There were exigent circumstances." She shrugged.

He closed his eyes and let out a long sigh. "That's not how 'exigent circumstances' works," he said. His voice had quieted to a low rumble.

"Pfft! Who cares? That's how you're gonna say it works if anybody comes asking. But nobody's gonna come asking." She jerked her thumb in the direction of the media room. "That right there? That's drugs off the street, money on the table, and that's a big photo op for the front page."

B-Girl put her feet up on her boss's desk, tipping the chair back beyond what would look safe to Morella, but Camille felt the perfect balance inside of her. "Maybe some of those high profile arrests won't stick, but it's not like some crime boss is gonna sue us to get their money and drugs back citing improper procedure. The only person who's griping about this is your ambitious ass. C'mon!"

"What's that supposed to mean?"

"We all know that you're trying to make political moves. You wanna be the chief. Chief wanna be the mayor. Y'all ain't fooling anybody."

"What I do with my career is none of your business," he said, but he suddenly shifted his weight uneasily.

"It's my business when you out there in front of the cameras using *my* bust to puff out *your* chest. As long as you've been here, you've been zero help, man. But you keep moving up the ladder. That's fine. Play it how you feel. But don't expect me to smile and nod when you're passing around credit for *my* work only to come back here and tell me that I did it wrong."

"You think some good press overrides the need for proper procedure?"

"You're goddamn right it does! And if you disagree, don't tell me. Tell those reporters. You don't need that good press, go back out there and give it back." She kicked back off the desk, got up from her chair, and walked to the door. "Tell me when I've gotta meet the review board for this bust or leave me the fuck alone and enjoy your moment in the sun." With that, she left and slammed the door behind her.

She smiled as she walked through the station, heading for the exit. Her whole body was sore and ready for sleep. Press conferences happened during the day and this was way past her bedtime. Crossing the station floor where the other superhuman agents worked, she spotted a red-haired reporter furiously scribbling notes while talking to

Double M. The reporter hastily finished their conversation and jogged over to intercept Camille before she could leave.

"B-Girl! I'm Cassidy Grant from *The Cargill Question*. She/her. Do you have a second to talk about your big haul from last night?"

Camille hadn't spoken to the newspaper in more years than she cared to remember. The idea of a reporter leaving Double M to talk to her was completely unfathomable. "I mean, I'm heading home. So maybe just a second."

"Thank you. I'll be quick." The young reporter thumbed a button on her phone, then flipped the page on her notebook and began scribbling again. "Major Morella said you were the point person on last night's action. Care to elaborate on what your role was?"

The truth, of course, would get Camille into trouble. It was time the higher-ups understood that she could play the political game as well as they could.

"While doing routine street-level patrols, I spotted some local big names coming and going from that discount electronics store. After a week of casual observation, I brought it to my superiors and the major gave me the go-ahead to enter the store as a customer and report if I spotted anything out of the ordinary. Unfortunately, the thugs working there identified me as a cop and tried to engage me in a hostile manner. I had reason to believe there was active and ongoing criminal activity happening on the premises. It was definitely exigent circumstances. One hundred percent. I had to act in order to keep any further crime from happening and to keep any evidence from being destroyed."

"Wow! And you weren't expecting such a huge result, were you?"

"No, but when you got the support and expertise of the brass like Morella and Double M, there's no reason not to approach every situation confidently. Whether it was a big bust or a small one, I knew they had my back."

"That's great to hear. I won't take up any more of your time. This is front page news and I'm glad the *Question* got a chance to speak with you directly."

The reporter hustled off to make her deadlines and Camille paused to take a breath. Out of the corner of her eye, she spotted something purple. She turned her head to find Double M fully armored and leaning against the door frame to her office. She was looking directly at Camille with the faintest of smirks across her face.

It's good to know I'm not just amusing myself out here, Camille thought as she resumed her path to the exit.

Chapter 15

Vanessa

I ended up deciding not to quit my job. It was a fun fantasy, but reality held me back. Fortunately, reality was pretty fun too.

I don't know who B-Girl called to get an exclusive that night, but every local news station was all over the bust—*our* bust. I sat on my bed watching my now-favorite superhero talking about the good we'd done for the community. I wondered how long it would take before these clips ended up on *For Hire*'s website. That would put *me* on the website, as well. Unnamed, unseen, and uncredited. But whenever they mentioned the amount of cash seized, they'd be referencing my first contract as an operator. That number was light by two hundred thousand dollars and nobody knew except me, B-Girl, and Rey.

My favorite part was during the police department's press conference. Hearing the street value of the drugs that were taken in possession was almost as surreal as meeting Dawn Taylor had been. Just under half a million dollars? I didn't know the inner workings of the drug trade, but it was still essentially run like a retail business and I'd worked retail jobs for years. An enterprise large enough to utilize several distribution centers could probably function with the loss of a single location, but it would still be a hit to their profits and their ability to resupply. Most importantly, that all represented product off the streets. B-Girl said we'd be creating a positive effect on Cargill and we had. I figured she only brought that up as an added bonus to the amount of money we'd be raking in. Turned out it really mattered to me.

All morning, I kept my TV on and sat at my desk with my laptop open, reviewing the positive effect last night had had on my life. First off, I noticed that I had an email from the government's Extralegal Operations department. The subject line read 'Operation Complete - Five Star Rating - Payment Sent'. When I opened it, it was barebones, just like everything having to do with operators. No details and no names. All the email contained was a client ID number (689411), a single sentence stating that the work was marked as concluded, and two links. The first of the links was to the dispute office, in case there was a problem with the job or the pay. Everything I needed to know was in the subject line... and in the backpack next to my desk.

I reached down in its depths and lightly caressed the cash I had taken home last night. Getting paid in cash meant that I could either keep the paper money as-is or print a deposit slip from that second link in the email. The slip would contain a barcode linked to my contract details and my bank information. I'd be able to drop off my cash payment at virtually any bank in America. Whether I was a customer at that bank or not, my money would land in the account I had specified in my operator profile. Being an operator had interesting benefits.

Regardless of how I held on to my newfound gains, with twenty thousand dollars in hand, I could consider re-enrolling in veterinary school, or moving out of my dad's house, or both. The numbers didn't play out on the latter and I, of all people, knew it. I could use this money to get something started, but I could never finish that something. Twenty thousand wasn't a home. It was a down payment. Twenty thousand wasn't a degree. It was maybe two or three semesters toward one. My barista check wouldn't cover the remainder for either endeavor.

The realization made the joy of the moment drain out almost entirely. All of a sudden, I felt underwhelmed by my audition – or more accurately, the five-figure payout that resulted from it. In less than a week, I went from being a barista with dreams of self-sufficient adulthood and a meaningful career to being right on the edge of living that dream. But that just wasn't enough. As ungrateful as I felt about my new situation, I couldn't shake the source of that feeling. I needed more money to really move the needle. And I wanted it, more than I had wanted anything in so long.

I opened a new tab on my browser and went back to the operator website. A couple of clicks later, I was logged in and staring at the pool of unclaimed contracts. I barely even knew what I was looking at. There were dozens of listings: Hacking. Kidnapping. Theft. I even saw one for an assassination. Some jobs required weeks of travel while others could be done from home in a matter of hours. They were sorted by classes but I didn't understand the criteria used to rank them. All I knew was that the few A-list contracts paid huge sums of money. Any one of those jobs could've covered at least half a mortgage in the best neighborhoods Cargill had to offer. But all of them had really stringent or complicated parameters. This was the work of the masters, *For Hire*'s ranking leaders.

Scrolling all the way down to the D-List jobs, I found work that I could do. Or at least thought I could do. I wasn't sure. The contract conditions seemed within my abilities to accomplish, but what if they weren't? The contracts didn't come equipped with a superhero safety net and mismanaging a D-List contract could lower my all-new status. Clients wouldn't employ an operator that couldn't handle bargain basement jobs.

Also, D-List jobs didn't pay a ton. Sure, I'd be able to make a fairly stable living from them if I completed at least one every week. I'd even be able to leave my coffee shop gig and become a full-time operator. But I couldn't trust that there would be a steady stream of well-paying jobs that also served the people of Cargill. There was a job listed as "freelance accounting" in Cargill today. But there was no guarantee of a similar one next week.

So, what I needed was work that I knew I could do but also had some kind of backup in place. I would require contracts that I could be sure would benefit the local neighborhoods, all while paying enough to accomplish my goals and still be worth the risk in the first place. The contracts were complicated, but my standards for accepting them could be too. Or maybe it was just easier to talk myself out of doing something scary.

That was a long thought process only to end up right back where I started: I needed to talk to B-Girl about doing another job.

I had ideas though. Both the ledger and the spreadsheet from last night had other addresses. Maybe one of them was another casino or some other type of illegal business. There had to be more money we could squeeze out of another front and more positivity we could spread to the people we lived around. I could put together a set of prospective takedowns and then approach B-Girl as a partner, not just a tagalong.

It was amazing how quickly I got recharged thinking about the prospect of getting back out there with B-Girl. I couldn't remember the last time I felt this enthusiastic about any task I set myself to do. I couldn't remember the last time I'd been this excited about anything that wasn't basketball.

Basketball!

Now *that* was an endeavor I could afford in full. The Gizmos were leaving town tonight to start a first round playoff series against the Miami Manticores but they'd be back in Cargill for games three, four, and possibly six. I did great last night. I deserved to splurge. I also deserved to show off to my dad that I was doing just fine.

That settled it. I opened a new tab and went straight to ShowGo. I didn't even have to search. My location settings already brought up the site's suggested events and playoff tickets were the hottest thing available. The very first item on the page was for game three on Friday night. Sure, I could've been responsible and waited until I deposited this money in the bank on Monday, but nope. I used my terrible credit card with the high interest rate and dropped a thousand a piece on a pair of courtside tickets right then and there.

Vanessa Copeland: Big Money Spender!

Chapter 16

Camille

By the time Camille got home from the police station, Rey was out and about. She didn't pause to wonder where he was. Instead she made a beeline for her bed and passed out almost immediately.

When she awoke, her husband's presence was instantly noticeable. The glow from the living room, the faint sounds of the television, and the light clatter of a keyboard all gave him away. Camille slipped out of bed. She moved quietly down the hallway and peeked around the corner to the living room.

There Rey sat, his legs up on the couch, alternately focusing on the TV and the computer on his lap. Thirty years together and she still loved seeing him at rest. As stressful as their life had been together, she cherished the few moments when she could see him by himself. He was almost a different person alone.

"Hey handsome," she said, leaning against the wall where he could see her. "Whatcha up to?"

"Solving problems, Cammie. Fixing thangs." He pulled his attention away from his screens and grinned proudly up at his wife.

"Meaning what?" she asked, perhaps a little too sharply. Camille sometimes wished she could go with the flow of her husband's enthusiasm, but far too often his fixes only created larger problems.

"I tried to pay off the bills with all the money you brought in last night." His smile wavered a bit, and his eyes searched her face for clues on the right way to proceed.

"What the fuck are you talking about, Reynolds? What do you mean you 'tried to'?" Camille left her spot in the entryway to stand directly in front of the couch and look down at him.

"Most of the billpay places that accept cash aren't open on Sunday. So, I paid off the one bill I could and came home to list out the rest of them. I've got every dollar itemized and a list of open billpay places to hit tomorrow. So, by Monday afternoon, we should be clear of a huge chunk of our debt."

Camille blinked twice then closed her eyes completely and inhaled deeply. She didn't want to yell, but she felt it coming. *First I've got to keep this fire from spreading,* she thought.

"Where's the money now, Rey?"

"Down in the basement. Still sitting in the duffel bag. Except for the little bit I already spent. Why? What's the problem?" He sat up a bit straighter on the couch.

"We've been teetering on the edge of broke for years and you think it's smart to drive around town with almost two hundred thousand dollars, paying off bills in cash? It hasn't even been 24 hours since *your wife* busted up a casino leading to a two million dollar cash seizure. What were you thinking?"

"It was an illegal casino. It's not like a bunch of drug dealers are gonna come looking for their money."

"The dealers won't. But Internal Affairs will. They can't spot us being so reckless with money they know we don't have." She touched her fingertips to her temples and prayed away an oncoming migraine. That would have to wait until this situation was contained. "What was the one bill you paid off, Rey?"

"The car. The dealership was open. So I went down there and cleared the note."

"We owed almost fifteen thousand on that note. If anybody asked, where were you gonna say you got fifteen thousand cash from? You better hope nobody notices that shit!"

"Then what are we supposed to do? We're still sitting on over a hundred fifty thou and you're saying we can't spend it? What then? Do we launder it?"

"Do you know how to launder money, Rey?" She couldn't keep the bitter laughter out of her voice. Rey looked back down to the laptop and began typing before Camille reached down and snapped it shut. Breathing out another deep sigh, she continued. "If I.A. even suspects me of doing some foul shit, the first thing they'll do is seize this laptop and find 'money laundering' in your search history. We gotta be smarter than that."

"I just want to come up with options. I don't know how money laundering works. If you do, then explain it to me."

"We would need to open up a business. As clean money comes in, we mix it with our dirty money, and by the time it gets back in our pockets, it all looks legal. But that's a lot of work that we don't know how to do."

"What about the kid? Number girl. She's gotta know how to do more than just add and subtract, right?"

"I already gave her ten percent of our money. I don't want to give her another ten just to allow us to spend what we're already holding. Plus, we would need to have access to a business just as a start."

"Don't we though?"

"Don't we what?"

"Don't we already have access to a business?"

Camille thought for a second and then it hit her. She fixed Rey with a glare that could melt steel. "I swear to god if you say his name or the name of that fucking restaurant, I will murder you. I will take this ponytail and choke you to death with it. Even Double M wouldn't find where I buried you."

Rey flinched, and he wasn't a flincher. But after a brief moment, he smiled, set aside the laptop, and got off the couch. Laughing heartily, he hugged her and lifted her off the ground.

"You thought I meant…? No! I meant you. You're a superhero. You're the business we have access to."

"Put me down and tell me what you're talking about." The anger faded from her voice as Rey literally swept her off her feet and spun her around in a dizzying circle. By the time Rey slowed down and let her feet touch the ground again, she was smiling as well. How did he manage to do that?

"It's just like when you were getting endorsement deals." She didn't stop to correct him on the use of plurals. "We just keep doing big jobs like last night's until the marketers start feeding the B-Girl brand again. Then we mix that new money with our old money and clear our debts. Boom! We don't have to hurry either. We can still just pay month-to-month while we wait for the faucet to open."

She thought about it for a moment before hugging him back.

"See? That's why you're my manager. That should've been the game plan from jump." She wasn't just shining him on, either. Sure, he made small problems larger—but he also occasionally made large problems smaller. Loving him was as easy as being annoyed with him. Sometimes even easier.

Chapter 17

Vanessa

It was amazing how long I was able to extend the excitement of the moment with a pair of tickets. I spent a week at work putting up with JoMo's bullshit with a big smile on my face. I was gonna see Dawn Taylor up close again and my dad was super excited to go to his first playoff game. Nothing could bring me down.

When we arrived at Wise Mechanics Arena, we knew we were extremely early. But missing any part of the experience was not an option, even if that experience was mundane until we got to our seats. The team had asked all the fans in attendance to wear team colors to create an ocean of blue throughout the stands. To help, each seat held a blue t-shirt with the team's playoff slogan, "Cargill Can!"

I already had my blue Dawn Taylor jersey on but I got up to go replace the black t-shirt I wore underneath it. Before I could, my dad nudged me and pointed to the court. When I turned around, I was face-to-face with my hero.

"Hey hey, if it isn't All-State Copeland." Dawn Taylor was just coming out of a jog while the rest of the team was still taking more laps up and down the hardwood. "So—are you here about that thing?"

It took me a second to understand what she meant. I knew her from a playing career, an autobiography, and a countless number of interviews. She only knew me from an illegal gambling den.

"Oh no! That thing is over and done with. I'm here about *this* thing." I raised my hands to indicate the entire arena. "I've never been to a playoff game. Wait! You know my name? Oh my God! How do you know my name?" I should've been worried about safety and privacy, but I wasn't. All I knew was that my favorite ballplayer knew me by name and it felt amazing.

"I was curious the other night, so when I got in my cab to head home, I looked up recent city champions and all-state honors on the internet, and there you were. I even watched a little of your film on MovieMover. You were really good. I'm sorry you got such a raw deal. A talent like yours deserved better."

I couldn't feel my face but I assumed I was smiling from ear to ear. "Thank you for saying that. This is the single most surreal moment of my entire life."

"I'm sure it'll pass." Just then a whistle sounded and Dawn looked over her shoulder. Dawn! My inner monologue was on a first name basis with her now! She gave her trainer a nod and turned back to me. "Warmups are about to start, though. Enjoy the game. Cheer real loud."

"Thanks. I will." And then I did it. Before she ran off and before I could stop myself, I blurted out, "Trav Parker always jab-steps before he shoots a three. He never just comes up off the dribble. Never!" She didn't respond. She just smiled, nodded, and joined her teammates in the layup line.

"Soooo... you know Dawn Taylor and you couldn't be bothered to introduce me?"

I winced. I had forgotten my dad was even there. Could you blame me?

"How do you two even know each other?"

"It was part of that freelance accounting job that I mentioned. I didn't know it but she was a client of the company I was auditing. She just happened to be in the office when I passed by and we talked ball for a couple minutes. You know how it is when you run into other sports fans."

"Yeah, I guess I do."

Ugh, I was getting a little too good at that lying thing. Before he could continue the conversation, I patted him on the shoulder and bolted to the restroom to change my shirt.

Fortunately the start of the game, which I timed my return to perfectly, soft pretzels acquired, kept him occupied.

By the fourth quarter, the game was well in hand. Cargill was crushing Miami in part due to some uncharacteristically strong defense from the Gizmos' star player. The local celebrities, who only really attended games to be seen, were all heading to their limousines. Dad and I were still front and center and edge-of-our-seats excited.

In a futile effort, the Miami coach called a timeout to try to stop the Gizmos' momentum. As Dawn Taylor walked to the bench, she glanced directly at me and smiled. I was convinced that she was thinking about the great defensive stops she had made using my information about the Manticores' star player, Trav Parker. And maybe she was, because the next second she looked at a tall man a few rows behind us and mimed writing on paper.

When the man stood up, Taylor called out "Front row. Braids. In my jersey." I didn't know how to respond to that. The tall guy did though. He was next to me and crouched at the edge of the court so fast he could've teleported. He was right in my dad's face but didn't acknowledge him in any way.

"Hey," he said. "I'm Marcus Gonzalez, Dawn's assistant. She'd like your contact info so she can reach out to you sometime after the game."

"Um, sir," I straightened up in my seat. "Are you asking me to be a groupie? Because, yes! Absolutely yes." My father glared at me. I didn't care. If this was my moment, I was taking it. Unfortunately, it was not.

Marcus laughed. "No, sorry. She just wants to be able to reach you. Usually it's because she has something to say but no idea when she'll have the time to say it." He handed me his notepad and pen then leaned in a little closer. In a hoarse whisper, he said, "We actually have a different signal worked out for the groupies."

I laughed to hide my disappointment, then wrote my name, cell number, and email address on his notepad. He thanked me and was gone before the whistle sounded to resume play.

Now maybe it was the overconfidence of an impending blowout win, maybe it was the beer, or maybe it was the sting of him getting ignored by her for his own kid twice in just a few hours, but Dad started getting mouthy about my BFF Dawn.

"Taylor is so impatient. She never takes enough time to let a play develop. She just brings the ball down court and comes right up off the dribble as soon as she's got any breathing room at all. Her step-back jumper is ugly, too. It's even uglier than yours. She's always off-balance. If my J was that ugly, I wouldn't be letting it fly so free."

I queued up my usual response of *Yeah, Dad. I know*. But this felt like it crossed a line. It wasn't that he called my jump shot ugly—it was. Hers was too. It was that he felt like he needed to criticize what worked. Part of me felt like that had always been his problem. When I was a star player, it was at the wrong position. When I was an awesome daughter, I wasn't a son. I knew he worked at it, but sometimes I needed good enough to be good enough.

"She's not off-balance, Dad."

"Huh? Then why is she always on the floor?" My words barely registered and his eyes didn't leave the court. He didn't know we were arguing yet. He was about to find out.

"She's lighter and faster than most of the players that guard her. She can get in position for her shots before the defense can. It's why she always has enough room for that step-back. But defenders rush in to cover the distance and almost always make contact. If she leans off-balance, it's easier for her to flop and draw the foul. Yeah, she's always on the floor, but she's always on the free throw line too. She's ninety point six percent from the stripe. She knows exactly what she's doing."

His eyes flickered to me. "You're just mad that I called both of your jumpers ugly. Don't be salty about it. It's just my opinion."

"I won back-to-back city championships with an ugly J. She led her team to the playoffs three years in a row with an even uglier J. Maybe your opinion isn't as important as you think."

Even uglier than either of our jump shots was the way I punctuated that last sentence by shoving the last half of a hot dog in my face while staring down the man who raised me. He was looking at me full on now, seeing me.

I loved my dad. But standing up to him felt good.

Chapter 18

Camille

When the kid arrived at Camille's door three weeks after the job, music was flooding the house inside and out—classic R&B from the 1970s and 80s, the soundtrack to every family barbecue. She was immersed in memories, and moving slowly, which was to say, not at all. Rey made it to the door before she even registered the doorbell, but from the loft upstairs she could hear the exchange.

"Hey, li'l mama! Got a taste of the life and now you hooked, huh?"

There was a pause. "I have no idea what any of that means. Is your wife here?"

"She upstairs."

In the loft, the music blended with the faint sounds of the television. Camille was sitting on the couch watching *Top O' The Morning* with the captions on and had decided for sure she wasn't getting up. She was out of uniform but didn't care if the kid saw her. She was looking fabulous in a gold satin cami and matching panties under a long silk robe. Her ex had called it "celebrity-wear" and used to joke that the only things missing were a pool, a deck chair, and a pair of high-fashion sunglasses.

"Hey," she said when the creaking stair told her Vanessa was close enough to hear. "You're ready to work again?" Despite the interruption to her day off, Vanessa coming out on her own put a smile on Camille's face. Maybe she wasn't the only one who needed another job to happen.

Vanessa looked as awkward as ever, shifting in discomfort, but her voice was steady as a rock. "Yeah. If you're into it. The money from last time was great. But it wasn't enough to really change my situation, you know? I'd need this to be a more regular thing if I'm gonna eventually get out of my coffee shop job."

Camille had a lapse in focus and began staring at Vanessa. And staring, and staring.

The kid finally burst out with a nervous "What?"

Camille shook her head. "Look, what you're saying is important and all that, but your edges are fucking me up. Come sit on the carpet over here."

She got up off the couch and went into the next room as Vanessa settled in. When she walked back in, she was holding a cosmetics case. She sat back down on the couch with a leg on either side of Vanessa's body. She opened the case and pulled out a spray bottle.

"Wait! What are you doing?" Vanessa asked.

"Ya mama didn't teach you to refresh your edges?" Camille asked as she sprayed water on the loose hair that had grown since the last time Vanessa had her braids done. The mist from the bottle got in

104

the kid's eyes and she tried not to flinch away from Camille's hands. "While I do this, tell me about the thing you do with the numbers. How's that work?"

Settling in a bit, Vanessa seemed to take a second to gather her thoughts. "Have you ever used a spreadsheet program?" she finally asked.

"Unfortunately, yeah. My ex-husband and I used to do the household budgets together."

"Okay, so you know how you can use a formula to do some of the math for you? And then the cell turns red when the numbers don't balance?"

"Sometimes we got more red than not when we'd budget," B-Girl responded without thinking as she took thick dabs of leave-in conditioner and worked them into Vanessa's new growth one braid at a time.

"That's just how my mind works when I look at or hear numbers. I don't even work at it. I just take in the numbers and they either make sense or they don't. And if they don't...."

"Red cell."

"Exactly. So then I can figure out what's wrong with them and fix it. In the case of what we're doing, I know almost immediately what figures are unaccounted for."

Camille never had much patience for young people, even when she was young herself; she always felt like they asked for more than they were offered. This felt different, though, settling in with Vanessa like this. Camille felt strangely fulfilled by taking care of her, just a little.

After this, the kid would know how it worked. They were doing for each other. She could build a friendship with terms like those.

"What about you though?" Vanessa raised her eyes to look up to Camille. "How's... body control work?"

Camille shrugged as she slowly retwisted each braid along Vanessa's hairline. "I read people's physical intention and can adjust my body to dodge or combat it."

"What does that mean, 'physical intention'?"

"Like trends, but in motion. When the body moves like *this*, I can tell it'll eventually move like *that*. But that's the weird thing about GVS. It doesn't make any sense. I've met people who could read motion when it came to objects but were lost in a fight. I'm the other way around."

"So you're invincible in the ring but a liability on a dodgeball team?"

"Not completely in either case, but I got my limitations. I've been overwhelmed by too many people to read at once. I've fought variants who were too fast for me to dodge or too strong for me to block. But I can go into most one-on-one fights knowing that I'll win. It's just like you and your abilities, though. I don't work at it. It's a reflex. The best boxers in the world train for years to be able to read and react the way that I do. And I can do that with any part of my body."

"The sex must be incredible," Vanessa exclaimed, then looked mortified. In response, Camille tugged on one of her braids. "Ow!"

"Don't get fresh. But yeah, the sex *is* incredible." Camille laughed, and Vanessa eventually joined in. As Camille finished twisting the last few braids, Vanessa picked up the bottle of conditioner and took in the name. From the case, Camille retrieved a small tub of styling gel and a toothbrush. Lightly dipping the bristles into the gel, she laid Vanessa's baby hairs down into place along her hairline. She pulled out a satin scarf like the one on her own head and tied it across the edges she had just tightened.

"There. That'll keep you looking fly for a little while longer."

"Thanks, Camille. That was actually a first for me. My mom—she's been gone a long time."

Impulsively, Camille leaned forward and gave Vanessa a hug that the kid held onto a bit too long before she suddenly withdrew and reached into her backpack to pull out a folded piece of paper.

"These are addresses that I saw on the ledgers back at the casino. There were more, but these are the ones I remembered. I meant to bring them to you sooner but JoMo's had me on a different shift so I didn't see you and I wasn't sure.... Can we do another job?"

Camille took the paper and examined it. She moved her lips as she silently read the four addresses, taking a brief pause to think after each one.

"I know all of these," she said. "A couple of them are QDB construction sites. Ya know, Quinn Design & Build? They put up maybe a third of the buildings over in the business district."

"Does that mean anything to us? Why would a building still under construction be a stash spot?"

"It's only short term. The foreman or whoever is probably letting gangsters use the construction site to hide some of their cash and/or product for a while. There's lots of plausible deniability if shit goes wrong. If shit goes right, the foreman gets two paychecks for the same job while doing almost nothing to earn the second one. If it doesn't…. Well, it's in his best interest to make sure it does. What that means to us is that it's a temporary drop on a spread-out piece of land. Finding anything on plots that big are a dice roll. You might find a fortune or nothing but wet cement. It's not even worth scoping out." She pointed at the third address on the list. "This one here is a bar, though. Figgy's over on DeWise Avenue. It's a tough joint, but nothing we can't handle."

Vanessa grimaced.

"It's nothing *I* can't handle, kid. We'll scope out the place and figure out what the danger is. If there even is any. Your audition's over."

Chapter 19

Vanessa

Just like last time, we had a stakeout—several, actually. The bar was a far more active target than the electronics store had been. But just like before, we picked the perfect time to strike. Unlike the casino, we didn't expect the count to change drastically with the time of day or the day of the week. That meant hitting the place at its least busy would be best: Tuesday night around 7 p.m.

We sat in the backseat of Rey's SUV until we spotted a single driver approaching. He hopped out of a double parked sedan, carried a striped duffle bag into the bar, then drove away without the bag a few minutes later.

"This is it. Same as last time. I roll in and handle the crowd. You follow close, lock the door behind us, then head to where they keep the stash. The layout in the bar is a lot more spread out than the casino was. It still shouldn't be a problem." B-Girl forewent her aluminum bat for a satchel full of thick metal posts.

I was feeling keyed up, but good. B-Girl was confident that we could shake down this storeroom without disrupting the bar that hid it

109

and I believed her. I was looking forward to seeing her in action again. Kinda fangirling over the idea, really. The way she had moved in that casino was unbelievable. I absolutely wanted to see how those posts were gonna be used. I might even have been embarrassingly eager when Rey passed them back from the front seat, but oh well.

I couldn't keep the excitement from my face as I left the SUV. I rushed in close behind her and locked the door immediately. When I turned, though, B-Girl wasn't in action. She was just standing near the door staring at the bar.

"Of course it's her," she muttered.

I followed her line of sight. Behind the counter stood a tall black woman with long dark hair tied into a tight braid kind of like B-Girl's but far shorter. She was pouring herself a drink. A quick glance around revealed that the room was empty except for the three of us.

The tall woman took a sip of her drink, put down the glass, and vaulted smoothly over the counter. I took in her appearance. The first thing I saw were the boots—black, steel-toed, and heavy, but worn, with gravel between the treads. When she landed, I saw that she wore dark brown pants with several pouches on the hips. I could only wonder what was inside each one. Her sleeveless white t-shirt clung to her body and did nothing to hide a pair of leather gun holsters over her ribs. The holsters were empty, so my eyes instead lingered on the ripple of her biceps and forearms. Now that she was simply picking up her drink and moving towards us, I could tell that her strong physique was the kind that came from extensive physical training.

"Welcome to my parlor." She walked slowly between the tables while keeping her eyes dead on us. And I'm not kidding about the dead part—this lady had shark eyes.

"Teresa," B-Girl said, with a steely calm. She hadn't moved an inch. Through her jumpsuit, I could see her muscles tensing. Was this one of the people who was too fast for her? Is that why she wasn't kicking ass already?

"Camille," Teresa replied, almost casually. She positioned herself directly between us and the path to the back rooms. The intention was clear. To get paid, we'd have to go through her.

"Are we gonna do this?" B-Girl spread her feet a bit and bent her knees slightly. She was ready. I was ready!

Teresa took another sip. "It's fair to say that fighting isn't really in either of our best interests tonight."

"Why are you here then?" I actually saw a drop of sweat fall from B-Girl's hands. This was a woman who took down goons in waves, so yeah, now I started to freak out a bit.

"I'm here to discuss something that *is* in both of our best interests. I mean, we can fight if you really want to, but that's not gonna get you paid."

That's when she looked right at me. "You're the sidekick right? Her pet accountant?" I nodded. I resented being labeled a sidekick. My audition period was over! But not knowing who this woman was, and without a signal from B-Girl as to what to do, sure, I'd play the sidekick. I kept my expression as blank as I could. Vanessa Copeland: Intimidator.

"What you're looking for is in the back. Second door on your right, just past the restroom. Do what you're here to do while the grown folks talk."

I looked at B-Girl and she turned her head slightly to nod, never taking her eyes off Teresa. I cinched my bag further up on my shoulder then headed towards the back, walking just past both women.

"Take only what's there for you," Teresa said in a low, scary voice as I got near. I looked up and saw that she never took her eyes off B-Girl either. As much as I wanted to continue watching their epic stare-down, I was here to do a job. I could faintly hear them start to talk as I went through the door.

Not gonna lie, I thought about stopping for the bathroom because I felt like I was going to pee myself when she talked to me.

When I entered the office, the setup was similar to that of the casino: racks loaded with cash and taped-up bundles of drugs. Maybe the movies were right and that was just the most efficient way of storing these things. When I found the computer, it was already unlocked and logged in. At the casino, we busted in while work was still being done and surprised them, so it made sense that we had access to the computer. This time, no one was back here working. The terminal should've logged off on its own well before we arrived—unless we were being given access this time.

How had they known we were coming?

The math took even less time than before. The files that I needed were already open, the ledger was already turned to the correct page, and the exact dollar amount of excess already sat right next to the

112

computer in the striped duffle bag we just saw being delivered. This wasn't a bust. We were being given this money. But why? Was it a trap?

I was sweaty now too.

Maybe it was a paranoid step, but I took all the money and flipped through each stack before stuffing them into my own bag. I didn't even know what I was looking for, maybe a sensor or a paint bomb or something. Either way, there was something special about the breeze on my face from fanning fat stacks of cash, and I was chock-full of conflicting emotions as I did my part.

I exited the room and went back out to the main bar. When I got there, B-Girl sat on a stool holding a drink of her own while Teresa stood behind the bar again. They both stopped talking when I approached.

"We're not done here yet, kid," B-Girl said. "Wait for me in the car and I'll be out soon."

I nodded and made my way to the door. Something told me that the less I spoke around this Teresa woman the better.

Once out of the bar, my body relaxed a little but definitely not completely. None of this made sense. Why would we be welcomed in and allowed to leave with money if Teresa had the power to stop us? If she was an enemy, why was B-Girl having a drink with her? There was so much I needed to ask about but—*puppy*!

Sadly, the adorable Labrador was wearing a service dog vest, so I resisted the desire to pet and reluctantly moved my eyes to the owner. Okay, also appealing. They were good-looking as hell, with light blue eyes that were exactly at my level. When I pulled my glance away, I noticed they had a bag with a DiNapoli's logo. Now that I could feel things other than tension again, I realized I could go for a sub. I wondered how long B-Girl would be.

"You can pet him," said the owner. "I'm good. Stand down, Stephen."

The dog visibly relaxed and approached me to sniff. I put out my hand. He was so soft and good.

"Hey, I'm Bobby, he/him," his owner said, extending a hand.

I nodded, ignoring it to run both of mine over Stephen's coat. "Vanessa. She/her." Too late, I wondered if it was a good idea to give a stranger my real name during a job. But what was I supposed to say? Before B-Girl and I got started on this whole endeavor, I had changed the name on my operator profile to Vanguard. But giving him that name probably wasn't a good idea either.

I needed an operator handbook.

"Good to meet you, Vanessa, but I've got a sub to deliver." He nodded to the bar.

"Uh, I think it's closed," I said, which I realized a second later was probably more information than I should've given. I was not good at this. Handbook, *please*.

"It's cool. I know the owner," he said with a heart-jumping smile. Damn, he *was* good-looking. He pushed the door open and went in, leaving me to stare at the curl of dark hair at the nape of his neck and the happy wag of Stephen's tail.

Okay then.

Chapter 20

Camille

Camille was not happy with this turn of events. This was supposed to be an easy job where no one got hurt, but instead she walks in and there's Teresa fucking Blackwell. She tried not to flinch as the kid walked right past her. Too close. When they heard the office door close, she spoke.

"How's the knee?" She kept a straight face. Of course she did. Teresa Blackwell knew how to walk the line; she'd been in the game her whole life. You didn't spend decades successfully navigating the Cargill drug trade without being a lot of things to a lot of people. Sometimes she was deadly, other times charming. She could be absolutely calm or completely unhinged. Today, Camille couldn't tell if she was legitimately concerned or simply gloating.

"Once the brace came off, I was walking straight again. I didn't even need surgery," Camille said as she narrowed her eyes. "How's the concussion? Still sensitive to light?"

Teresa tensed up and grimaced. If it was a battle of wills, this would've indicated a loss. It was something else though: camaraderie. Fake? Real?

"I wore sunglasses everywhere for almost two months before my vision finally readjusted." She walked back to the bar and indicated with a vague hand gesture that Camille should follow her. "The scars on my back never quite faded away though. The people I fuck ask if I got branded."

Camille smiled at that.

"Speaking of which, how are things with you and what's-his-name? Matt something?" Teresa vaulted back over the bar as she said it. This time, it was Camille's turn to flinch. The score, if there was one, evened.

"That ain't funny, bitch. If I thought you came anywhere near him..."

Teresa laughed. "Relax, Camille. Nobody wants your sorry-ass ex. Now tell me what you're drinking and let's talk."

The two women stared daggers at each other across the bar. But who was Camille to turn down a free drink?

"Keep it simple. Rum and Coke. No ice."

Teresa pulled a glass from under the counter before reaching to the top shelf for rum. "You robbed us the other day." She poured an unchecked measure of rum in the glass with her right hand and used the soda gun to fill the glass with cola with her left. "The casino? That was my employer."

"And what? You expecting an apology?"

"Obviously not. But you're here, too. Are you targeting us specifically for your little smash-and-grab operation?"

Something about the way she said operation set Camille on edge. "I don't know what you're talking about."

"C'mon, Cam. Your bosses announced the total count on the news and we know we lost two hundred grand more than that. Our cameras picked up your little friend leaving with a bag before the news crews arrived." Teresa smiled. It wasn't a nice smile.

"Great. You can put two and two together. Now what?"

"Now nothing. The footage of your friend has disappeared. You're welcome." She took the last sip of her drink and refilled while continuing. "I've had you followed since the casino. We figured out that you were targeting this place. That's why I'm here. Plan A was for me to come down here and fight you. This is Plan B. But I've got to know whether or not this is some personal vendetta against my employer."

Camille made a face. "Teresa, I don't even know who your employer is. This is a stash house and I came to bust it up. It don't matter to me whose stash it is."

Teresa's smile widened. "That's great, actually. That means it doesn't matter where you get your money from or what you bust up to get that money."

"What are you talking about?"

"In a minute, your little friend is gonna walk out here with another two hundred thousand dollars. Then you're going to head down to the harbor over in Hawkins, dock number four. You'll find a rival operation bringing in a huge shipment. That's where your bust is."

"Are you kidding? You're bribing me to protect your employer? As if I can't just hop over the bar and beat that ass?"

"Look around you, Camille. This isn't a casino. There aren't any businessmen or politicians here to arrest. It's just us. Everything we've got in the back? Fake. Play money and powdered sugar, paid for out of my own pocket. The only real money is what's waiting for your pup. You call this in and you'll look like a fool." Teresa leaned forward. "There's fame to be had, but it's down at the harbor."

Camille gave it some thought. "And what's to stop me from busting up another one of your employer's places after?"

"I guess we'd go back to Plan A. But this ain't that kind of bribe, Cam. I'm not buying your loyalty—I'm renting your attention. I'm hoping you and I can have another conversation after today. One that's *not* on my employer's behalf."

In the silence that fell, they heard Vanessa's footfalls approach. The kid returned holding the bag cinched up high on her shoulder. Her hair looked great. She looked like she might die of nerves, but she was still doing her thing. Camille felt a flash of pride.

"We're not done here yet, kid. Wait for me in the car and I'll be out soon," she told her. Vanessa nodded then headed out the door. Camille turned back to Teresa, who was now scribbling a note on a bar napkin.

"Why should I trust you?"

"That's not company cash she's carrying. That's my own money you're leaving with. When the boss sees his bar still operating, his interests secure, and you all the way out in Hawkins, it'll be assumed

118

that I miscalculated your trajectory. That's part of my job and I'll look as if I'm bad at it. I'm taking a loss right now just to talk to you."

"All this just to recruit a cop?"

Teresa scoffed. "Let's be honest, Camille. Once you left that casino with our money, you crossed over to my side of the line. I'm just offering you a bit of guidance now that you're here."

Camille took another moment. "We've been at each other's throats a long time. But here you are pouring me a drink, handing me six figures, and offering me better prospects? What is this? What are you getting out of this?"

"Let's just say that you're not the only dog who's never gotten her day, B-Girl. Maybe I'm tired of us putting each other in the hospital. Maybe I'm tired of sacrificing my body for someone else's fortune altogether."

"Oh, but you're gonna sacrifice my body for it, then?"

"Trust! I've got a lot to say about that part of the equation too."

"Oh really?"

"Yes, really. But I can't talk about it now. Go to the harbor. Dock 4." Teresa slid the napkin across the bar until B-Girl picked it up and gave it a look. On it was a name and two sets of numbers. "That's what you're looking for. Though I can't guarantee it, there may even be more money in it for you. You must leave right now. This opportunity won't be there in a couple hours. And after, when things settle down, call the second number on that napkin."

Camille stood up, downed the remainder of her drink in a single gulp, and said "I'm gonna see about this and then I'm gonna see about you. If this isn't on the level, we're gonna have a different conversation than the one you want." Then she stuffed the napkin in a pocket and walked towards the door.

Just before she reached the entrance, it opened ahead of her. A young man walked in holding a bag from DiNapoli's in the same hand he pushed the door open with. Following close behind him was a black dog that Camille scootched to avoid. As she walked through the door, she heard his voice over her shoulder. "It's dead in here. Where is everybody?"

She let the door close behind her. In front of her was Vanessa, still holding the bag full of money.

Chapter 21

Vanessa

B-Girl burst out of the door a second after Stephen and his human went in. She placed her hand on my back—a light touch, but the urgency was clear.

"We gotta go, shorty! I told you to wait in the car. Why are you still standing out on the street?"

"I met... never mind. Where are we going? Who was that?"

B-Girl waved down the block and Rey quickly drove up to meet us. She turned her head back to the bar briefly before jogging to the car, opening the back door, and nudging me in. "We're heading to the docks in Hawkins."

"That's your hometown, isn't it? What's there?" She shut the door behind me and got in the front passenger seat. After closing the door, she finally responded.

"I cut a deal back there. If we tried to shut down that place like we shut down the casino, we'd have had a fight on our hands. One that maybe wouldn't have gone so great for me." Holy shit, I'd been right. Imagine someone who could take out B-Girl! I wondered what her powers were. "Instead, Teresa hooks us up with a different job and we leave with the unaccounted-for money, just like we planned."

"Okay. But then... your bust doesn't happen." I didn't exactly know how to word what I was trying to say, which was something like, *Hey B, aren't you in it for the money* and *the fame?* I felt like I should know her intentions better, if we were going to keep working from my list.

"A bust *is* happening. A much bigger one, supposedly—down at the docks." She spoke those last four words directly to Rey, who got her meaning and made a left to get on the parkway. She turned back to me and added, "Technically, that money you're carrying is payment for another job."

Money was good, but an unknown location was not in my comfort zone. "It's not a trap, right? We can trust her?"

B-Girl shook her head. "We can't trust *her*, but we can trust what she's *about*. She scores a two-fer here. First of all, she looks like she kept her boss's stash house running. The only money we took is money that wasn't officially on the books anyway. Second, we knock over this next place and it weakens her boss's rivals. For us, though, it's more shine and hopefully even more money. We gotta move fast though. Time is tight on this one. I don't even know if we're gonna get a second paycheck, but we're gonna try for one."

I thought about it for a while in the back of Rey's car. It might be more money but it wasn't what I signed up for. Wait—like, literally!

"This isn't the contract." With the music bumping and her distracted, she hadn't heard me. "Camille! I've got a contract and this isn't a part of it. If we're being careful, I need a contract for this too."

"What, like right now?"

"It takes at least forty minutes to get to the docks. That's long enough for you to get on your phone, close out the current contract, and write up a fresh one."

B-Girl groaned but pulled her phone out anyway. "I've got the app. I'll just knock that out. Be ready to accept it as soon as it comes through."

There was silence, and tapping, and in the boredom of the car ride something hit me harder than I expected. "You didn't correct that woman."

"What are you talking about?"

"When she asked if I was your sidekick. You didn't correct her."

Camille scrolled. "I was preoccupied. Why are we talking about this? Your feelings hurt?" I couldn't tell if she was mocking me. I hoped she wasn't.

"Back at your house, you said the audition period was over. That makes us partners. Partners get half."

"We don't even know if there's money at this thing."

"Fine. But if there is, I want half."

"Twenty-five percent."

"Why would I accept less than what I deserve? Half!"

"I'm doing all the fighting! Sixty-forty?"

"You wouldn't be able to skim a single penny if I wasn't for me. Even split!"

She huffed, but I got the sense she was pleased. I was learning the fine line between her annoyance and her respect, and I was pretty sure it was where you took something that should rightfully be yours.

"Fine. I'll add it to the contract."

She tapped her fingers on the screen of her phone for a little longer, then my phone buzzed right as we hit the red light at the end of our off-ramp. I had three notifications. Two of them were new emails from the Office of Extralegal Operations and the third was a friend request on Podville. Confused, I opened the latter first and was greeted by a photo of a Labrador. The text beneath the image read "Stephen says hi!" Underneath that was the name Bobby Quinn Jr. and two buttons marked Confirm and Delete.

I didn't realize how much I was smiling until B-Girl said, "Yeah you're a partner now. Confirm that shit and let's go." I confirmed the friend request quickly before tabbing over to my email. Both unread messages had the same client ID number (689411) followed by the rest of the subject info. I skipped the five-star confirmation email for the bar job and opened the request for the dock job. I didn't need the description but I skimmed it anyway. *Freelancer needed to balance books for a small, independent enterprise.* I confirmed my acceptance of the contract and dropped the phone into my bag.

After a few twists and turns, Rey had us approaching the shipyard. "What are we looking for?"

"Dock 4. I've got a ship name and a container number. Blackwell says it's cargo that's being unloaded right around now." It took a while to get all the way to Dock 4. The remote location was probably intentional. The best way to move illegal products was to keep far away from general traffic. But also it was a good way to trap someone. I still didn't trust that shark-eyed woman and I wasn't going to until this job was over.

It was getting dark but Rey kept his headlights off. Arriving here had to be as secretive for us as it was for the criminals. We followed the faint light of the streetlamps and the illuminated digital signs indicating each dock number. Eventually, we spotted a board listing the ships currently docked. Several of the slots were blank, for empty docks. While the listing for Dock 4 was also blank, a quick glance told me that the dock actually held a Panamax-size container ship with a fair bit of activity surrounding it.

They looked busy, so maybe it wasn't a trap?

B-Girl threw the satchel with the metal rods back on. I guess I was finally going to see what it could do. She stepped out of the SUV but leaned back in to address me.

"These guys have guns and the distance to use them. I'm good, but you should wait 'til the coast is clear, then follow up. Rey, you wait in the car too." She blew a kiss to her husband, slammed the door, and turned to face the danger.

"You're about to see something," Rey said. I don't know if he meant to ease my nerves. His words just heightened them instead.

Chapter 22

Camille

B-Girl only went a few steps away from the car before she broke into what she called her Big Danger routine. It'd been years since she'd had to use it, but for her it was like riding a bike. She produced a pair of wireless headphones from her pocket and pushed them into her ears. From another pocket, she pulled out her phone, adjusted the volume to just above a whisper, and searched for her playlist. She was already bopping her head and bouncing back and forth on the balls of her feet in anticipation. To face large groups of armed men she had to get in the zone.

Someone else might've gotten over the slight of not being called to aid the other heroes during the disturbance at Pierce Park in the month that had passed. More than enough time had gone by to get over the resentment of not having an endorsement deal renewed. Anybody else would've found a way to process and progress past the annoyance of all the minor affronts she'd faced over the years, but not Camille. She needed to channel that kind of ongoing frustration. It fueled the focus she needed for a massive undertaking like this.

The parking lot sat about a hundred and fifty yards uphill from the dock. The path down was wide and ended at a roadway that led left towards a freight yard of shipping containers stacked three high—a virtual maze of metal with thirty-foot walls. To the right of the roadway was the dock holding the CSC Axion, the ship Camille was targeting.

The calm before the storm was her favorite moment during busts this big, and she tailored her Big Danger playlist to that effect. Starting with a jog at the slow guitars of Babe Ruth's "The Mexican," Camille had broken into a sprint by the time the beat picked up. Mid-run, she counted a dozen guards positioned near and onboard the Axion. Undoubtedly there were more that she couldn't yet see. That meant she had to clear and move as quickly as possible all while finding protection on the run.

I can be quiet, she thought. *I can be quiet, but I need them to be loud.*

Running directly towards the boat would've left Camille exposed to incoming gunfire both from guards on the shore but, more dangerously, from those on the boat itself. They'd have the high ground. That wouldn't do at all. Instead she veered left, far away from the ship, before cutting through the relative cover of the stacked containers. If anyone spotted her from the boat, she would be able to hear the commotion of armed enforcers preparing to face her. Instead, she heard nothing but the faint music.

Of the guards that Camille could see, half of them were stationed near the maze of cargo. Judging each one's line of sight, she found a straggler she could pick off. She ran at him. He didn't stand a chance. By the time he heard the footsteps, Camille was on him. He swivelled to look at her but found himself being swung face first into the nearest container. He was out.

Unfortunately, the container was too full. She was looking for the loud, attention-grabbing echo that an emptier unit might have provided. Peeking around the corner of the maze's nearest intersection, she saw only one guard cautiously drawing near. His hand was on his gun and he was tentatively glancing over his shoulder. He lightly thumbed his radio but didn't speak into it. Instead, he began slowly creeping towards Camille and her unconscious prey. *You don't wanna alert your boys until you confirm the threat, huh?* Camille thought. *Don't worry. We're about to confirm it together.*

As the guard came around the corner, gun first, she grabbed it and yanked it forward with the muzzle pointed down and away from her body. He didn't let go but Camille was counting on that. Angling her body and twisting, she gave the guard two choices: either let go, allowing her to disarm him, or hold on tight and let himself be pulled into firing the gun involuntarily. He chose the latter. It was the obvious move.

The sound of repeated shots finally drew the attention of the entire security team. A spotlight shone down to the cargo yard from the Axion and the other guards moved to meet it. By the time they reached her position, they'd find two of their group knocked out, several dismantled gun parts, but no superhero.

Camille had already slipped off into the darkness, leaving the criminals wary and in need of communication. She gave her enemies confusion and in return they gave her tactical data—their guns were knockoff MP5s, cheap and easy to get, the kind of gun that made expendable soldiers look and feel badass. If these guys had been real professionals, they'd have better weaponry... and they wouldn't be so crowded together. The smart move would be to split into two-man teams and spread out their search. The spotlight should've be roving inward instead of outward. They were amateurs, but still deadly ones.

It was easy for Camille to avoid the remainder of the ground forces. They all just followed the spotlight as it slowly panned towards the parking lot. A few quick cuts through the container maze brought her behind the whole team with nothing between herself and the ramp onto the Axion.

Camille spotted one guard leaning on a railing at the top of the ramp and watching the gathered forces in the distance. Three more guards were visible on the ship's deck, the last of which was manning the spotlight. They all had enough room to effectively fire on her, but only if they saw her coming.

The music changed to "It's Just Begun" by The Jimmy Castor Bunch. Camille took that as her cue to break into a run for the ramp. Finally reaching down to her satchel, she slipped out the first of the six heavy steel rods and launched it with a backhand motion. Opening her fingers, she activated the tech in her gloves to add a magnetic push to her throw. The rod flew just past the first guard's head as intended. Surprised, he only had enough time to draw away from the rail and look over his shoulder before Camille clenched her fist to pull the projectile back. On the return flight, it connected with the guard's temple and knocked him over the railing he'd been using for support. He was unconscious before he hit the water.

By the time the rod returned to her hand, Camille was almost at the top of the ramp. With the height of the fall, no one had heard the splash or the impacts of the takedown itself. Looking around, she was pleased to see that her initial count of four onboard guards was correct. But the lighting was dim, so she didn't want to be so cocky as to not take a lap to be sure of her surroundings. She used the magnets in her gear to climb to the top of the onboard metal containers. From that vantage point, she could see all three guards below her on the deck and the ten she left ashore.

The boat must've docked hours ago, she thought. *There's no one else here. No crew. No witnesses. It's all just armed goons here to secure whatever the merchandise is. Sixteen total and I've only cleared three. It's fine, I can take my time as long as they're still searching the yard for me.*

As if in response to her thoughts, the other guards on the Axion began speaking excitedly in a language Camille didn't recognize. It started as loud chatter before exploding into full-on shouting and pointing.

Looking down to the deck, she saw the spotlight being raised up the path until it illuminated Rey's SUV parked in the lot. In the distance she recognized Vanessa standing on the car's roof.

Those damn fools! I told them to stay in the car!

The guy operating the spotlight opened fire on the two non-combatants. Vanessa hopped down to the far side of the vehicle and Camille could see Rey help her back inside. The SUV was bulletproof and submachine gun fire wasn't a major threat at that range anyway.

But the same could not be said about the shore team, who were already moving up the hill to the parking lot.

It was definitely Big Danger time. The song changed to "Apache" by the Incredible Bongo Band. Camille got a running start before jumping down to confront all three guards at once. She landed atop the closest enemy and launched a steel rod at the next nearest. While she incapacitated the first guy, the rod didn't hit its mark as effectively. She'd only knocked the man back a step, so he was disoriented but still standing.

She had to throw a second rod at his dominant hand to stop him from recovering and returning fire. She closed the distance between them and put him down with a quick flurry of punches.

The spotlight operator heard the ruckus behind him and turned in time to see Camille charging at him. He had enough time to lift his gun but not to aim it before she leapt onto him. Like the earlier guard, this one let off several frantic shots as B-Girl tangled him up in both her legs and her long braid. The searchlight was knocked off balance and shone wildly into the night before coming to rest on the deck.

The team on the shore looked up to figure out why the light had changed. What they saw was a limp man fall to the deck as Camille removed her ponytail from around his throat.

Though the car in the parking lot was the easier target, Camille had now positioned herself as the most obvious threat. The remaining members of the security team turned back and raced towards the boarding ramp. If the ten of them could get aboard, they'd have her both trapped and outnumbered.

Camille wouldn't allow that. Flexing her fingers, she magnetically called the last two thrown rods back to her hands. She yanked her sleeve above her right wrist and retrieved the pair of hair ties she had waiting there. Using these, she secured a rod to each of the spotlight's two handles and quickly tested her magnet-tech's ability to manipulate the light.

She focused the beam on the incoming group of soldiers. As expected, each of the ten men held up their hands to shield their eyes. In a hurry to trap her in her corner position, they all rushed onto the boarding path at once. That was their last and biggest mistake. With their vision obscured, they didn't notice her new location directly in front of them at the top of the ramp.

Releasing control of the light but leaving it aimed to blind her opponents, Camille engaged in the first of ten brawls in a row. One by one, she rained mayhem down on each guard before sending them over the railing and into the water below. On the narrow ramp, they were crowded too tightly to fire on her without hitting one another. The guards in the front couldn't handle the barrage of punches Camille threw and she mowed through them too quickly for the guys in the back to exit the ramp and give themselves room to respond.

The final two men tried to run, but to no avail. Camille was on a roll and smoothly launched a pair of rods in their direction. Both men were struck and knocked flat. Flexing her fingers towards the rods one last time, Camille watched them both return smoothly into her hands. She returned them to the satchel at her hip and took a moment to bask in the glow of the spotlight and observe her work.

All sixteen criminals were down and the coast was clear. The danger was over and now the music felt obtrusive. She pulled the headphones out of her ears and stuffed them in a back pocket before pulling out her phone and calling Rey.

"Hey, my love. Were you watching?"

"Of course I was. You still got it."

"Oh, I know I do. Tell Numbers to come on out here. She's up. When I hang up, give it a few minutes, then swap out the SIM card in your phone and make an 'anonymous' call to the media and to my station to let them know where to find me."

"Your station too? Why?"

"There's a lot of fools laid out over here and even more in the harbor. I'll be damned if I'm cleaning them all up."

Camille hung up, took a deep breath, and walked over to retrieve the rods she'd affixed to the spotlight. A lot of good work was done, but there was still more to do before she and her new partner could call it a night.

Chapter 23

Vanessa

My hands were shaking when I opened the car door. I couldn't believe what I'd just seen. B-Girl had beat up over a dozen men in rapid succession, completely took them apart. But as amazing as that was, the thing that had my nerves on fire was that I had almost been shot.

Even with my powers, I couldn't tell how much of an exaggeration that was. My abilities lost accuracy when I was stressed and my panic was definitely factoring in. While my eyes told me that the shots didn't get anywhere near me and Rey told me that the car was bulletproof, my brain screamed that men with guns fired at me and tried to get closer to fire at me again. I was almost shot. I was almost fucking killed.

And what would happen then? How would this have gotten explained to my father? Scratch that. *Who* would've explained it to my father? When an operator died in the middle of a contract, the records opened up. B-Girl would've been identified as my client. According to the operator website, clients who kill their operators and vice versa were punished severely. I never read the part that explained what the penalty was if I simply died under my client's watch. Either way, my dad wouldn't want to know I was mixed up in any of this.

I had to get that stuff out of my head though. I already spent my one unprofessional moment standing on the roof to get a better look at B-Girl. I couldn't afford any more time to dwell on that near-death experience, not while I still had a lot more work to do. So I told myself my brush with death was just a distraction, a hindrance, a—a conflict of interest.

But my legs were shaky as I ran to the boat. It took everything I had not to lose my balance. I was even less sure-footed when I got nearer. I didn't know if I'd ever get used to having to step over all the unconscious bodies B-Girl left in her wake. I had to tiptoe around two of them as I made my way onto the narrow ramp that brought me aboard the Axion. I tightened my grip on the handrail. Being above the water where she dumped several soldiers made me feel a bit queasy. Were any of *them* dead?

"C'mon. This way!" Camille waited for me at the top of the ramp and waved me to the left. "Time's a factor. I want you in Rey's car and out of here before the cameras show up. And especially before any of my squad gets here."

I couldn't respond. I couldn't open my mouth at all for fear of vomiting. I just nodded and followed her as she led me up to the bridge. When I entered, I was surrounded by gauges and dials, none of which I understood the purpose of. My head was still spinning when B-Girl took my hand and guided me over to a station covered in ledgers, maps, and shipping manifests. I should've thanked her for that. I'd never have been able to find what I was looking for on my own.

"Here's the container number. Look through this crap and find our box." She shoved a bar napkin in my face.

It was exactly what I needed. Concentrating on numbers eased the mental strain of focusing on physical sensations. I wiped the sweat from my hands onto my jeans and started rifling through paperwork. My body felt better almost immediately.

I paused at every instance of the number B-Girl showed me. Some entries listed the container's origin—Hungary—while others were coded descriptions of the content itself. On paper, it was said to be filled to capacity with "recreational materials." *Drugs*, I thought. That made sense. B-Girl was about to make another huge bust, even bigger than the last one.

I found the container's location, still on the ship, unmoved. Before telling B-Girl, I searched for references to dollar amounts, payments, exchange dates, and so on. If there was money to be had, I'd find it. But then something else drew my eye.

Camille tapped her foot and leaned on the bridge's entrance. "Did you find it, kid? Is there any cash to skim?" I held up a finger to quiet her and kept flipping through the pages. I had to be sure of what I was seeing. There were names and indications of amounts owed. But these weren't purchases—these were debts.

"Oh my god oh my god oh my god! We've got to open it up. Run! Blue container near where they kept the spotlight." To her credit, Camille didn't ask any questions, just took off and ran straight to where I indicated. Meanwhile, I took one last look through the documents, hoping to be wrong. I needed something to contradict what I had read.

When nothing appeared, I followed B-Girl out to the deck. I caught up to her just as she used the magnets in her gloves to disable the lockbox securing the container's double doors. My eyes began to water as I noticed that those doors had holes drilled into them. I held my breath and B-Girl lifted the lock rods and pulled the right-side door open.

"What the fuck is going on here?" The illumination from the rising moon and still-functioning searchlight filled the container to reveal dozens of people staring back at us. Some were crouching, some standing, some sleeping huddled against the walls of the container. "Are these refugees?" B-Girl asked.

"They're trafficking victims. Sex slaves. The paperwork said they all owed a lot of money overseas. This gang bought out their debts on the cheap and intended to rent them out until they earned their freedom. But they never would."

"We ain't getting paid, are we?"

"No," I said, giving her an incredulous look. "But we have to do something about this."

"Something like what? All we can really do is turn 'em all in and hope they find a better life than what was waiting for them."

"Well, that's what I meant. But we can make them feel safer in the meantime. The documents said they were from Hungary." I whipped my phone out and opened the Comprendo app. I selected Hungarian and spoke into the microphone.

"We've stopped the ones who kidnapped you. More help is coming. Nobody owns you anymore." I held up my phone and raised the volume, then hit the Translate button. As my words rang out, translated to Hungarian, I could see the group relax. Some began to weep. A couple of young people, not much older than me, turned to relay the message further to those who didn't understand. I saw smiles and hugs and laughter.

Some of the laughter came from B-Girl, who threw an arm around my shoulder and said, "Look at you giving a fuck."

"A few years ago, a friend showed me a documentary about trafficking. After that, I studied the laws at play here. If sex work was decriminalized or just straight-up legalized, this kind of thing wouldn't happen. The only reason people feel like they can buy and sell humans like this is because none of us are allowed to earn our own livings doing sex work. There need to be safer avenues for this."

Camille just nodded. "Okay, Joan of Arc. I don't know how much I can realistically do. But I'll talk to some folks I know in immigration and see if I can at least delay having them sent back to wherever they came from. Maybe they'll get lucky."

"Thanks, Camille! I know that's probably a lot, but you'd be changing all of their lives. More than you already have, I mean." I hugged her and then stepped back to wipe away a fresh wave of tears. "Does it always feel this way?"

"It varies from person to person, I suppose. I can't remember the last time I felt like all of this," she pointed her finger at my face and swirled it around. I laughed and she laughed with me. "Alright—get out of here, kid. You've done everything you could and more than anyone could have expected."

I took one last look at the people finding their way out of the shipping container before heading back to the ramp. I was amazed at the turnaround in how I felt boarding the Axion versus how I felt disembarking. It would've been nice to leave with another stack of cash, but I still felt like a million bucks. And there was still ten percent of the money from the bar waiting for me in the back seat of the SUV.

The media vans arrived just as Rey pulled out of the parking lot. We passed the flashing red and blue lights of squad cars as we reached the freeway. B-Girl would need to debrief her fellow officers and show her face for the news cameras. In the meantime, I crashed hard in the back seat as Rey drove me back home.

Vanessa Copeland: Liberator.

Chapter 24

Camille

"Aren't you getting a little old for this, B-Girl?" a voice behind Camille called out. She'd heard similar comments before and had a stock response prepared. The words froze in her mouth as she turned around.

"You've gotta be kidding me. Laine Monteith?" Her face broke into a smile as she took in her old friend.

"Ahem! That's Captain Laine Monteith to you, Baston."

"So it is!" Camille glanced at the gold bars on Captain Monteith's shoulders. The two of them had worked together closely during the first two years of B-Girl's career but had long ago drifted apart. "Just a couple of kids from Hawkins making good, huh? But who are you calling old? You've been at it longer than I have. I'd have thought you'd hang it up before I did."

"Well, we're both getting close to mandatory retirement age." Laine shrugged. "My pension is secure, though. I can leave whenever I want. The only reason I stay on is... well, I still love helping people. I may end up as an unpaid consultant once they force me out." Laine

140

laughed in a self-deprecating way, but they weren't kidding. Camille could still see the passion for it in their face, something that had been lacking when she looked in the mirror for a long time now.

"Is that what you're doing here now, consulting? I'm a city hero and this is a big deal. The city cops are already on their way."

"So they are. But it's gonna take a while. They asked us small town constables to keep the news folks at bay until they arrived. You know, as a professional courtesy."

B-Girl was always acutely aware of when she was being managed. The only reason one department would allow another one to encroach on their superhero's crime scene was to keep an eye on that hero. Though she appreciated seeing an old friend, she bristled at the implication behind their presence. But she had to hide that for now.

"Why don't you show me what we're looking at here, Camille?"

B-Girl gestured to the captain to follow her onto the ship. "There's not much to show you. We found a shipping container full of trafficked foreigners."

"We?"

"You know, the royal 'we.' The Cargill police department, for whom I'm an individual agent." She let that sink in for a second. "Anyway, I set up a perimeter around the boat to keep the media vultures away. I found some blankets and food in the storage room and distributed them to the victims. A couple of them have a little bit of English, so I led them to the restrooms and they've been going there in groups. Mostly though, they're just waiting for a medical team and a translator. Unless you've got the Comprendo app on your phone."

"I've got a flip-phone, Cam. Not a single app to be found. How'd you even come across the whole thing anyway? This is a bit out of the way, isn't it?"

Camille stiffened. "I was off-duty and I got an anonymous tip. I happened to catch a small fish doing small things and in exchange for his freedom he traded up for a bigger haul."

"Lucky break, then. What if he'd played you?"

She knew they were sincere but her hackles weren't going back down. "Just because I don't have a name doesn't mean I don't know a face. I recognized him. I've seen him around. If he played me, I'd just bang him harder the next time. Nothing lost but time."

The captain seemed to make a decision. "Looks like you've made a high quality bust here. My guys will clean up the mess if you want to get out of here. Like you said, your city cops are on their way. There's nothing more for you to do here that can't be managed in a morning debrief session after a good night's sleep."

And with that, it had gotten embarrassing. Monteith was essentially asking a first responder on a major crime to take a walk. B-Girl could come up with a long list of people who might want credit for her bust, but that list became much shorter when she considered who might have the power to call in the Hawkins police force to interfere. The list narrowed all the way down to the only three people who could get Hawkins's captain out to the harbor themself: the major, the chief, and her own captain, Double M.

Not that it mattered. The bust was clean, as far as anyone could tell. Doubly so, since Vanessa didn't find any money to skim. B-Girl had used her own translation app to ask the victims not to mention

142

Vanessa's presence. Even if they blabbed to a translator, it didn't make much difference. The only way the CPD could pull up records of operator activity in the area was if there were signs of impropriety—which there weren't.

"How'd you get out here, Camille?" Monteith spoke up again, interrupting B-Girl's thoughts. "Do you need one of my guys to give you a lift back to Cargill?"

She hadn't even said she was leaving and she was being shooed away. So many insults, and this one delivered by a so-called friend. But B-Girl wasn't lying down for any of them. "I'm fine, Laine. I'll make my own way."

Which was toward the assembled press. "B-Girl? Hey, B-Girl! This is your second big stop in as many months. How do you feel about it?"

She smiled pretty for the camera. "I feel fantastic about it, if I'm being honest. The treatment these people suffered is unconscionable. A lot of lives were saved today."

Now this kind of press I don't mind going half and half for. Good job, kid.

Chapter 25

Vanessa

The twelve-hour turnaround was incredible. When I'd approached the Axion last night, I was just short of terrified. By the time I got back into Rey's car, I felt like I'd made a difference. The next morning, I woke up early and felt amazing, like I had saved the world. Okay, not the world, but at least the lives of some real people. No wonder some variants became superheroes. What a rush!

I went downstairs for breakfast, which was becoming a regular thing, and my dad once again sat at the kitchen table like a grumpy troll who hid under a bridge and gave out morning lectures to unsuspecting travelers. I got my answers ready. Had I come in late? I had. Was it any of his business? Not at all.

"Working hard or hardly working?" The dad-est dad joke that ever dared to dad.

"Har har," I said, rifling through the fridge. "Working hard, actually."

"That late?"

"Yeah. After hours is the best time to look at the books. You don't get in anyone's way."

He gave me a long look. "It's paying well?"

"Were the courtside seats not an indication? It's going great, Dad. I might be looking for my own place soon. Even thinking about saying goodbye to JoMo's permanently." I grinned at him. "Get me out of your hair."

"I don't mind you in my hair, Van." That fucking name again. It was harshing my good feelings. So was this whole conversation, actually.

"I'm twenty-two, Dad. Gotta move on sometime."

He took a moment. "Well, that would be a move in the right direction. But make sure you do the math."

I gave him the most incredulous look I could, for someone who couldn't raise her eyebrows independently. (I bet B-Girl could.)

"You've been trying to wedge me into boring entry-level accounting jobs ever since I left school, Dad. You already know I do the math. To be honest, it's one of the few things you really acknowledge about me."

"Well...."

"It's under control, Dad," I interrupted him. I wasn't expecting an apology and I didn't need a rebuttal. "Trust me. I've got it under control."

I'd been saying some approximation of those words to my father for years, but that time it finally felt honest. Even with my powers I couldn't map out what was coming next, but I was moving forward with confidence. Last time I did that, I was holding a basketball.

But I didn't want to dwell on that. Instead, I took my breakfast to my room, where I could analyze my future prospects in peace. I wondered if I could move out like I told my dad. Because I could *do the math*—which I was still salty about him saying—it was possible with the money I had. It really was. But it wasn't enough to feel safe about it.

Getting ten percent as an auditioning sidekick was great, but I'd need that renegotiated even split if I wanted to make any real changes. A half share of either of our paid gigs would've gotten me my own place. A half share of both would've gotten me a whole new life. I was on my way. I just needed to hear back from B-Girl about our next move.

Speaking of B-Girl, her smiling face greeted me when I flipped on my television. Given the color of the sky behind her, the footage was from last night. Over her shoulder I could see several officers helping people off the Axion. My heart swelled when I thought the feed was from a local station, but my jaw dropped completely off of my face when I spotted the North American News logo in the corner. Our little bust had gone national!

I dropped my plate onto my desk and grabbed a pillow from the bed to scream into it at the top of my lungs. The last thing I wanted was more questions from Dad, but my excitement couldn't be contained. I sat on the bed instead of at my desk to get closer to the TV.

"Can you confirm that this was a trafficking ring you shut down?" an offscreen reporter asked before pushing the microphone in B-Girl's face.

"I can confirm that it's at least a piece of the puzzle. There's no telling how big this is. That's what makes this stop really frustrating. The guys I put away tonight are bad, but so are the laws in place that make their business viable." She flipped her long ponytail over her shoulder and looked directly at the camera. "If sex work was decriminalized or just straight-up legalized, this kind of thing couldn't happen. The only reason criminals feel like they can make humans a commodity is because people aren't free to earn their own livings doing sex work. There need to be safer avenues for this."

My own words said back to me. Every part of this gave me goosebumps.

"Are you thinking about championing that cause, B-Girl?" a second offscreen reporter asked.

"One thing at a time, y'all. The first step is to make sure these folks ain't sent right back to the bad situation they just escaped." With a wave, B-Girl walked away and the camera panned to the first reporter. Across the screen, the crawl read *B-Girl Busts Up Trafficking Ring.*

"That was veteran superhero B-Girl just moments after taking down sixteen alleged kidnappers and saving the lives of twenty-six people allegedly captured as part of a human trafficking enterprise. North American News will keep you updated as this story unfolds. Reporting from Hawkins, New Jersey, I'm Saga Lowe."

Twenty-six lives altered for the better, in part because of me. I couldn't wrap my head around all of it. A little more than a month ago, I told Camille that I refused to make my life marginally better while supposedly helping some faceless population. Now I was sitting on the means to make my life dramatically better while looking directly at the faces of the people my work helped as they walked across the screen just behind the reporter. I couldn't take my eyes off them.

I'd helped do this. I could help people.

Chapter 26

Camille

"Who says you can't teach an old dog new tricks?" a voice boomed as Camille crossed into the area reserved for superhuman officers. Looking around, she spotted the purple hair and huge form of Double M standing in her office's doorway and looking right at her. Was her cheesy-ass grin genuine? Camille was never sure.

"That is, unless that old dog is Camille Baston," Double M continued, "and that new trick is real police work!" There was an outburst of laughter, which Double M joined. "For real, though, everybody give it up for B-Girl!"

The office erupted in applause, unpowered cops and superheroes alike. Even people that spent years badmouthing her were whistling and clapping for her at their captain's word. Struggling not to blush, Camille took off her hat and gave a brief wave, honestly moved. It was the only standing ovation she'd ever gotten. As the cheers died down, Double M motioned for Camille to come into her office. Camille put her hat back on as she crossed the bullpen, entered the office, and closed the door behind her.

"Sit down, Camille. We've got a couple things to go over." Double M held out a hand to indicate the seat in front of her desk as she took her own seat behind it.

"Thanks for that, McKenzie. You're a real class act." Camille sat down and got comfortable.

"You deserved it," Double M said as she picked up two large file folders. "These busts? They're spectacular. Lots of scumbags out of the game, lots of drugs off the street, lots of people saved, and a ton of money on the table. With the kind of photo ops you're providing, do you know how many higher-ups are making their careers off these busts?"

"I feel a 'but' coming on."

"But... a lot of those same higher-ups think you're dirty, Cam." Double M's expression was unreadable.

Camille jumped up from her seat. "Oh, here we go. Another fucking railroad job starring B-Girl. Y'know what? Fuck you, Double M. You're over here doing the brass's job for them? You can't take these busts away from me." She slammed her hands down on the desk. The captain, of course, was unphased by the outburst.

"Relax, Cam. Nobody's eating your kills." She held out a hand and indicated for Camille to retake her seat. "Major thinks you're dirty and the chief agrees. As the captain of the superheroes, they brought me in to discuss it. I went to bat for you. I went to bat for these busts." She placed a hand on the folders again. "They don't like you, but you already knew that. There's no evidence that these busts aren't clean. So I told them there was no way I was signing off on them treating a thirty-year veteran like a criminal on the strength of a bunch of old grudges. They didn't like that, but I carry a lot of weight around here. If I back you, you're backed."

"So we all good then? You know my cases are clear?" Camille sat back down warily.

"Let's just say there won't be an investigation into the finer details. We're processing them as if they're as perfect as they appear. But the only thing clear is that the major and the chief think you're dirty... and I'm inclined to agree." Double M waited for the angry reaction on B-Girl's face to return before continuing. "I don't think you're on the take, Cam. You're too goddamn stubborn to be in anyone's pocket. But my intuition tells me that something here isn't above board."

Camille thought for a moment before choosing her next words. "So why'd you go to bat for me then?"

"Can I be real with you, Cam?"

"As real with me as I am with you."

Double M smiled at that. This smile, Camille was sure, was genuine. "Unlike the rest of the department, I actually like you. You're hard-headed and self-important and you've been shitty to me more often than not, but I've always respected your resilience and self-assurance. Nobody can tell you anything, and that's at least as admirable as it is frustrating to work with. But that's only half of it." She took a deep breath. "I'm going through some... relationship trouble right now. It's got me out of sorts. I'm okay when I'm hitting things, but when I'm not fighting I'm usually crying. I just can't focus on this administrative bullshit, it's all politics and background noise. So, whatever game you're running? I'm not gonna bother sniffing it out. I don't have the patience to. As long as the right people are being punished and this stays a good look for the department, I'm going to make sure no one else bothers to sniff it out either. In exchange for my lack of diligence, you're going to keep your little side-hustle well hidden. Shit rolls downhill. As long as I don't have to deal with shit, you won't either. But whenever your hot streak wraps up, you're going to take me out for a drink and tell me what the real story is. Deal?" Double M stood up and extended her hand.

Camille stared at the hand for a moment, then stood up. "So if you weren't going through relationship trouble, then what?"

The captain met her eyes and spoke coolly. "You know me, Cam. If I had the time and the inclination, I'd find the truth and bury you with it. But as I said, as long as the right people stay away, I'm willing to keep Internal Affairs off your back. Do we have a deal?" She extended her hand a bit more.

Camille ran a quick pro and con list. Having the backing of the country's top hero would go a long way for her rising career, but being beholden to Double M didn't work for her. Neither did admitting to any corruption.

"I don't need your deal, M. My busts are clean. Are we done here?" The captain shrugged and withdrew her hand. She didn't seem surprised.

"Not quite," she said with a sad smile. "Tomorrow, stay home for your next shift. I'm giving you the night off and moving Stafford and Lawson over to cover for you. In the meantime, a writer from *For Hire* is coming out to your house for an interview."

Camille started. "What? Why?"

"They're coming up on their thirtieth anniversary and they don't cover enough older heroes. Not the active ones, anyway. Part of me going to bat for you was making sure you got all the accolades you deserve for strong police work. You're the star of the moment, B-Girl. Don't go fucking it up."

Chapter 27

Vanessa

Have you ever been a part of something big? The highs are really high, but the lows end up being surprisingly low. This was that second part. It'd been a little over a month of nothing—well, practically nothing. Definitely no more big somethings.

There were little somethings, mostly coming by way of email. I reached out to B-Girl about the possibility of working again and had gotten back a single sentence reply *I'll get at you when I'm ready.* I read the words over repeatedly and they annoyed me more each time. It wasn't even the money. B-Girl had been branded as a champion for sex worker rights based on my perspective. You'd think she could muster up more than seven words for the person she owed her newfound popularity to.

It didn't help that she'd stopped coming into the coffee shop. There wasn't even her daily visit to remind me that I was someone who made a difference in my other life. I was Vanessa Copeland: Restless Barista all day long.

At least there were good little somethings. I'd received an email notification from *For Hire* magazine. My work with B-Girl netted me three 5 Star ratings on B-list contracts in under two months. Turns out that's a noteworthy way to start your career as an operator, and I was being mentioned in an upcoming issue as a result. Weirdly, the email didn't ask for any input from me. I couldn't clarify my name—which I had just changed again—and I couldn't decline the mention either. Not that I would have. I would've liked the option, though.

Also appearing in my inbox were direct contract offers, three in the last two weeks. My impressive start didn't just get the attention of *For Hire*. I also popped up on the radar of local clients looking for workers. Even though the job details were sealed, employers could see that I worked in Cargill and did "freelance accounting"—that's how B-Girl listed it on my contracts, anyway. So that's what people wanted me for. I guess I was officially an accountant. My dad would be proud. Maybe. I don't know. I didn't open the emails. I read the subject lines and put them all in a file for later.

I knew I was supposed to be happy about all this. Instead, I was still trapped in this awkward space between having control of my life and being a stuck kid struggling to make it.

I also couldn't get settled with the idea that Camille controlled the path forward. Working with her had been a dream, but what if I never heard from her again? Would all this end up as a footnote in my boring autobiography, unread by anyone? *Let me tell you about the time I made a little bit of money before going back to being a shiftless layabout.* No. I couldn't accept that.

It was times like this when I wished I was still with Elise, who never stopped searching out new options for her career path. Maybe she could've helped me brainstorm a few for mine.

On my bed, alone with my thoughts yet again, I glanced at my phone for half a second and considered picking it up before it pinged on its own accord. Thank goodness.

I looked over to the screen and saw I'd received a new chat request on Podville. Since I already had my laptop open, I pushed my phone aside and went straight to my browser. The onscreen notification read that the incoming request was from Bobby Quinn, Jr.

With everything that had gone on with B-Girl and the job and the new cash, I had forgotten about the handsome puppy I met—and also their human. I was eager to talk to him again but I didn't want to seem desperate by responding right away. Instead, I skipped over to the open tab that contained my email. Vanessa Copeland: Smooth Operator! Get it?

I had already read or deleted most of my incoming messages. The only ones left were the contract offers that I had been a little too nervous to open. I clicked on the first one and scanned a very brief job description. It had a few lines of detail, but my eyes were drawn to the date at the bottom. According to the email, I had a week to accept this offer before it would be re-listed publicly. It had been twelve days. The same was true of the next offer, only it had been nine days since I received it.

Sure, I could go to the job listing website and see if either of the two contracts were still available, but the third email was much more interesting. It had arrived in my inbox only this morning and was marked

TIME SENSITIVE. I clicked it and waited. And waited. And waited. For whatever reason, this email took longer to load. I was sure it would only take a few more seconds, but I was impatient. I went back to the Podville tab to learn about Bobby.

According to his profile, his full name was Robert Quinn, Jr., he was twenty-seven years old, and he worked as a Development Manager for Quinn Design & Build. I was sure that wasn't a coincidence. I had heard of Robert Quinn, Sr. but I hadn't given the name any thought. Bobby Sr. was the construction king of the business district. So, I guess I met the construction prince. I wanted to see what His Highness was about. I clicked the chat window.

—-

10:14pm

Robert "Bobby" Quinn, Jr.: Hey, thanks for connecting with me.

Vanessa Copeland: It was for access to Stephen pics. :) :) :)

Vanessa changed the nickname for Robert Quinn, Jr. to Bobby.

Vanessa changed the nickname for Vanessa Copeland to Vanessa.

—-

The swirling icon on my other tab disappeared, which meant the email was finally done loading. I switched tabs and skimmed the contents. Almost everything I'd absorbed from the administrative side of extralegal operations had been static and boring so far and I was expecting more of the same here. Boy, was I wrong. Once finished, I scrolled to the top and reread the message carefully.

***

Greetings Operator #3683/VanTage:

Thank you for reading this. I'm going to give you as much information as I can. We work for a government agency. We think there's something wrong with our budgetary numbers and that there has been for a while. We don't have the skillset to uncover what the problem may be and we worry that those with the requisite skills may be at the center of that problem. We didn't know who to turn to, so a concerned few of us pooled the cost of hiring an operator. Your recent local successes spoke to us and we hope that you'll help us as well.

We can't tell you who we are or how we gained access to these documents. If we could have gone through the proper channels, we would have. We need an answer soon as we vote on a new budget next Wednesday. We can't afford to pay you much but if you uncover the discrepancies we believe to exist, we may be able to work out a bonus when the upcoming budget passes.

Thank you,
Client #719300

What kind of cloak and dagger shit was this? They gave me almost nothing, but I was into that. Below the text was an expiration date of midnight. I needed to decide on this job quickly—but I felt like I already had. I clicked the link at the bottom of the email, not entirely sure where it would take me. A new tab opened and the dry, lifeless design of the extralegal operations website appeared before I was redirected to an overview for the contract.

It didn't say much beyond what I already knew. Accepting the terms would give me access to a set of compressed files. It would also trigger a two-day deadline by which I'd need to report my findings. Declining would plop the contact onto the job listing board where it was likely to die. I didn't expect another local contractor to show up before the job's deadline.

The payment was five thousand dollars, way less than I'd made (or could make) working with B-Girl. But I was uncertain about that arrangement, and I was too new at the game to scoff at this kind of money. I clicked Accept just as my chat tab pinged.

I switched over to resume my conversation with Bobby.

—-

10:20pm

Bobby: That's understandable!

Bobby: What are you doing tonight? I'm just sitting here with Stephen curled up by me. I'm about to order from Inferrera's.

Vanessa: I'm just gaming. Don't order the special.

Bobby: Why not?

Vanessa: A couple of weeks ago, there was an oil leak in a boat in the harbor where the fish are farmed. They said they caught the leak in time but I wouldn't trust it. At this point, you're looking at contamination on a level where it's definitely going to affect the haul, so the special's going to taste funny at best, get you sick at worst.

Bobby: Thanks! You usually keep track of local seafood? :)

—-

I probably gave him too much information there. It wasn't exactly like I could turn off the way my brain worked. Sometimes it was intentional and other times I randomly absorbed lots of loose info. I couldn't remember where I saw the news about the oil leak and I had no clue when I learned about Inferrera's fish supply source.

I switched tabs back to the contract. In all honesty, I meant to distract myself long enough to come up with an excuse for why I knew so much about local fish or to let the topic drop altogether. What happened instead was that I reread the mysterious message and then clicked on the link to the files that my new anonymous employers had provided. It would take a bit to download. I switched back over to Bobby and purposely derailed the conversation.

—-

10:30pm
Vanessa: Sorry, I had a boss to defeat and had to turn on the mic and coordinate with my team.
Bobby: No worries. I wasn't trying to interrupt your night. But Stephen and I would like to see you again, maybe when you're not trying to do something else?
Vanessa: I'd like that.
Bobby has sent you meandstephenselfie.jpg
Vanessa: I see you got your late dinner. You about to fall asleep on the couch, old man?
Bobby: We party hard. How about subs at DiNapoli's sometime next week? About 7pm? Best day for me is Tuesday or Thursday.

—-

A tone sounded from the other tab: the folder was done downloading. For a second, I assumed the quick turnaround meant it didn't contain too many files. I was wrong. When I switched back over, I saw that, while the documents were all text, there were hundreds of them. I chose one at random and found myself staring at a budget for bookshelves. A second file presented an itemized list of computer terminals and related resources.

Was this for a library? No. The numbers were massive. It would have to be for the city's entire library network. More reasonably, it had to be for the city's entire public school system.

I was a graduate of Cargill's public schools. Even with some ups and downs, I still looked back on my experiences there fondly. Sorry, Bobby. The contract had become personal. I couldn't let myself stay distracted.

Within a few minutes, I had over twenty documents open and I was bouncing between them while taking notes on a blank sheet of printer paper. Those opened files quickly got replaced by another twenty and so on. What I found after an hour or two was that most of the school district's budget could be easily accounted for. If there was a budget for X dollars' worth of supplies, I could usually search for and find a receipt for an equal amount from a supply company. No problem.

The issues arose when there was no tangible product related to a budget item. Some of the identifying data was redacted, and I suspected that was limited to in-school employees. But the district also employed tons of outside lawyers, contractors, and consultants. It was harder to get a bead on where that money went.

I decided to look up one of the consultants. I didn't know what I expected to find, but I punched the name Manjari Olds into the search engine. It returned the image of a pretty brown-skinned woman with long dark hair. It was the profile picture for her WorkedUp account.

According to her profile, she was a curriculum analyst for several school districts on the East Coast. Her job was to monitor for cultural biases in learning materials.

Aha! While it wasn't as easy to define, she also created a measurable value. If there was something funny happening with the budget, that value wouldn't exist. Using that as my logic, I looked up every outside employee and firm that the district had given money to in the last ten years. It took a long time, but that's when I found The Dixon Agency.

A quick web search listed only a single entry, a corporate website. That site was even more bare than the operator one. All it contained was a few stock photos and a statement of purpose: *A charitable fund to promote great work in the inner city.* It didn't get more generic than that. The site had no links, no addresses, and no employee listings. I tried to look up their public records and found nothing. This fund was literally nothing. But every year, it received an increasing amount of funds that had been diverted from other out-of-district employees.

If two thousand dollars were earmarked for renovations to a school's playground, nineteen hundred went to the contractors who did the renovations. The last hundred was written as a check to The Dixon Agency as a consultancy fee. There were cuts like that in almost every department. Even that Manjari person had gotten a two thousand dollar haircut she likely didn't know about. She probably just accepted an independent contract from the school district without realizing that more funds had been set aside for whoever filled the role than she received.

The Dixon Agency had taken the rest. It was fraudulent to the tune of several million dollars a year. With the city employees' names all blacked out, I couldn't accurately say who was directly responsible, but looking through the school district website gave me a few likely suspects. One way or another, whoever was signing checks to that fund was the root cause of why I'd been asked to fulfill this contract. They were most likely signing those checks to themselves.

And that's exactly what I reported to my employers along with the rest of my findings. They could handle the rest on their own.

The sun had risen and my bed was looking like a long lost friend. Before I crashed, I closed all the tabs on my web browser, save one.

—-

7:03am

Vanessa: See you Thursday.

—-

Chapter 28

Camille

It was uncomfortably warm in the restaurant of the hotel. Uncomfortably warm... and uncomfortably *pink*. The carpeting, the booths, and the curtains were done in shades from pale rose to candy apple. On a far stage, a band in pink tuxedos played a slow tune. *It's like Valentine's Day came and never left*, Camille thought as she spotted a shirtless man in fairy wings playing a harp. She was no longer sure she had the right address and approached the desk to ask before she spotted her appointment and brushed past the concierge without a word.

Teresa Blackwell sat in a booth with open curtains. As always, she wore a top that showed off her muscular arms; this time, a form-fitting black tank top. Camille noticed a long-sleeve shirt bundled up in the corner of the booth. It seemed she wasn't the only one who disagreed with the temperature.

"What the fuck is this place, Blackwell? Is this a first date or something?"

Blackwell casually looked up from her menu and responded, "Well, technically, I *am* courting you."

Camille raised an eyebrow but calmly took her seat across the table.

"Back when this place opened a few years ago, this was the go-to for romantic couples," Blackwell explained. "The idea was that if you wanted to get out of your daily routine but couldn't afford a trip somewhere nice, you'd come here."

Camille looked around doubtfully. "Really? This sleazy place?"

"Trust. This was the spot." Blackwell placed the menu flat on the table and looked around the room. "You'd soak in the romantic ambience and enjoy good food and drink at a steep discount, but only if you reserved one of the rooms upstairs. These curtains pull closed for privacy. You know, in case you want an after-dinner handjob before heading up to bang on a hotel bed that shakes when you put quarters in it."

Camille rolled her eyes and sighed. "Okay. But why are *we* here? We're not exactly a loving couple and, at the moment, I'm all good on discount food and discount handjobs."

"You sure you don't want something to eat?" Teresa asked, looking around for a waiter to flag down. "The steaks here are worth it and I'm buying."

Camille stared blankly in response.

"Suit yourself. Like I said, it was for loving couples back in the day. Since then, it's become more of a place for cheaters, online dates looking to screw early, and privacy seekers looking to handle business."

Teresa pulled the curtain closed. "These days it's one of the best places in the city to discuss sensitive matters without being bothered."

"Let's get discussing then. What is it that you want?"

"Our situations aren't too dissimilar—" Blackwell began.

"You don't know shit about my situation!" Camille burst out, her expression souring.

Blackwell paused, reassessing. "Fair to say. But it's easy to guess that whatever your situation is, money helps. I want you to keep doing what you've been doing, but with me choosing the targets. Same as at the docks. I give you huge sums of cash and you take down rival jobs that I decide on."

"And why would I do that? I don't need your help choosing targets. I've got the backing of the Cargill Police Department."

"Do you?" Blackwell asked in a light, almost surprised voice. Acting was not her forte, but it wasn't like it was Camille's either.

"Uh, yeah? This is my job, Blackwell."

"And who at the CPD is gonna have your back when they find out you've been stealing from crime scenes?"Camille tensed. *Not one damn person.*

"And what? You think it's easy money to pay me to hurt your enemies? Isn't that your job?"

Blackwell gave the smallest of shrugs. "Part of it."

"And by paying me to do your job, you get to be Employee of the Month while not lifting a finger?"

Blackwell shook her head. "It's not like that. I've got bigger plans." She paused, a little theatrically for Camille's tastes, and leaned in. "I don't mean to be an employee for much longer. This arrangement

165

I'm proposing is short term *but,* if you stick with me after that, you won't need to be an employee either."

"What's that mean?"

Blackwell smiled in a way that unnerved Camille. "My boss isn't in the best health. He has some time left, but everybody knows he's making plans for the end. The problem is that he's trying to pass off the family business to his worthless twerp of a kid." The smile turned into a sneer. Blackwell couldn't keep the disgust off her face.

"And you want his throne for yourself?"

"I've *earned* that throne, thank you very much. You're what, ten years older than I am? But we entered this game around the same time. As soon as I was strong enough to lift a gun, I was being told who to point it at."

"Don't pull that bleeding heart bullshit with me. What is this, an Afterschool Special? 'Innocence Lost: The Dangers of a Life of Crime'?"

"You know they don't even make Afterschool Specials anymore?"

Camille huffed. "What's your point, Blackwell?"

"My point is that I'm being skipped over for a child who's never gotten his hands dirty."

Camille almost laughed at that one. "Shit, maybe our situations *aren't* that dissimilar."

"That's what I'm trying to say! As far as I'm concerned, when the old man goes, his kid goes with him. A bunch of weakened rivals makes my transition to leadership a much smoother affair."

"That's where I come in," Camille realized. "I know police tactics and procedures. If I stay on as a consultant, I can help your new organization stay hidden from the authorities. I can tell you how I found you and keep others from finding you the same way."

"Exactly. You wouldn't even need a sidekick for that role."

Camille sat with the idea and finally shook her head. "That might be a bit too much for me. Skimming a little off the top and completely flipping the script are two different things. Being a hero has been my calling for almost my whole damn life."

Blackwell made a dismissive noise. "Please! You've been a superhero for *decades*, and what do you have to show for it? You've been on the other side for a grand total of five minutes and you've already got two major news appearances and more money than you've probably made in years."

And the upcoming *For Hire* feature. It wasn't nothing.

"Maybe your calling isn't your calling," Blackwell said. "Maybe you missed it and this is your second chance."

But. "It's not that easy. Plus, I don't want to just ditch the kid."

Blackwell blinked. "What's the situation between you and this child? Is she your daughter or something?"

"Nah, she's just a stray I picked up. She's good with numbers. That's how I was able to rob your casino without being noticed."

"She exploited our sloppy accounting?" Blackwell nodded with appreciation. "That's smart. But that's in the past. You can always take care of her by splitting what I pay you."

"It's not just money. I'm coaching her up, building her confidence. She's good at what she does. She just needs a little push."

"So, you find the jobs, do all the fighting, and take all the risks with your career? Meanwhile the kid shows up, does math, and leaves with what? Forty-sixty? Fifty-fifty? That doesn't sound like an even exchange to me." Blackwell paused and thought about it. "How about this: you would still need to appear to be hitting us, as well. Our rivals can't know that we're working together. Occasionally, I'll quietly arrange some softer and safer opportunities for you to 'take us down' and you can bring your pup to work with you. I'll even botch the accounting myself so she can feel useful doing math that fills your pockets."

Camille didn't love it, but she did like it—at least enough to try it out. She could always throw Blackwell to the force if it didn't go down right. She'd figure out the details of how that might go later. For now, the money alone made it worth it, but having a role for Vanessa sealed the deal.

"That works. When do we start?"

Chapter 29

Vanessa

"Check ball!" Malik barked.

I didn't believe in providence. Or destiny, or fate, or whatever you'd want to call it. I processed the world in such a cause-and-effect way that I couldn't possibly believe in a predetermined destination for our lives.

"Here you go," I said back, flipping the basketball to Malik and dropping down into a defensive crouch.

When you could see the world the way I did, the lines that held it together became visible. There *was* no coincidence when you could spot the subtle trends and events that led us from moment to moment. So, I didn't believe in providence. But there we were.

Malik always dribbled the ball so hard I felt sorry for it. It was like he was trying to punish the concrete. I'd tried handling the ball the same way and could barely control it. I didn't know how he managed it. He didn't even look for the other four players on his team before he turned away from the basket and began backing me down the lane all the way from the free throw line. He didn't always play this physically, so I guessed he was taking the game personally. That's how this was going to be.

You see, Malik was my ex. Wait. No. That sounded dismissive. Malik was a lot more than that. The two of us came up together, met right here on this court. Pierce had always been a rough neighborhood. Our parents warned us not to come out here. But if you wanted to play ball against real competition, Pierce Park was where you went.

You couldn't be soft either. If you showed up here, you had to be able to ball or you had to be able to fight. Malik and I made this place home as long as our parents weren't looking. I was clearly the better of the two of us, but that didn't matter because we were a team. With me as point guard and him at the two, we were the city's most feared high school backcourt for two years. That is, until I began my transition.

Once I decided to openly identify as a girl, the school moved to accommodate me. That meant immediately placing me on the women's basketball team. They were decent. But 'decent' doesn't win back-to-back city championships. I put up great individual numbers, but never saw the same levels of team success.

Worse than that, when the teams evened out, it put me and him at odds. The girls' team got better while the boys' team got worse, and all of our respective energies got poured into improving our circumstances. Malik and I went from being inseparable teammates to a pair of buds struggling to stay connected.

What set us even further apart were our future prospects. When pro basketball became gender-integrated there was a severe and unforeseen impact on the competitive level of the college game. The only way to solve that problem was to integrate the college game, but that took years to do.

Once that happened, there was a severe but not-so-unforeseen impact on the way high school games were scouted. Ultimately, the only way to fix *that* imbalance was to integrate the high school game. That took years as well. In between those gaps, there were girls like me.

Playing together, we both would've gotten Division 1 scholarship offers from the best schools in the country. Without me, the holes in Malik's game got exposed. His offers were limited to less prestigious local schools—but at least he got them. I fell through the cracks completely. College scouts were still trying to manage recruitment across multiple genders equally. Women's programs like mine fell to the wayside. I failed to generate interest pretty much because no one paid attention to my games at all anymore.

Without a scholarship, my dad couldn't afford to send me to any of the Division 1 schools where I might've had a chance of walking onto the team. Because of my biology scores and extracurriculars, the only scholarship offers I received were to the veterinary schools I had also applied to. I watched my hoop dreams dry up. Malik, on the other hand, kept moving forward.

I tried to maintain our friendship after high school, but it was never really the same. We even tried dating for a bit to see if it would reconnect us. The sex was fun but the resentment was too high. He couldn't get over the fact that I was the better player. I couldn't get over the fact that he went further than I did despite that.

I hadn't played basketball in almost three years. I hadn't seen Malik in maybe two. We hadn't played on the same court since high

171

school. But all of a sudden, there we were. There *he* was, at a crossroads in my life, just like he'd been for damn near every other crossroads I'd encountered. I didn't believe in providence. Seriously.

The game went well. It was hard-fought. To the confusion of our teammates, there was a lot of hard-nosed one-on-one play between me and the guy I was guarding. They probably got that it was personal. But either way, my team won.

Playground pick-up rules said that my team stayed on while the losing team made room for the five players who were up next, but I was done. I wasn't really fit enough to run another five-on-five and I had other stuff to do. I grabbed my stuff and let my team replace me with the next bystander as I walked towards the exit.

"You're just gonna go without saying shit? You're just gonna show up, beat me, then leave like that?" Malik followed behind me. He had his duffle bag over his shoulder too.

"I'm not leaving. I'm just... leaving." He gave me a baffled and annoyed look. There was no look he could give me that I hadn't seen a million times, but it got to me every time.

"I don't know what that means. But we should talk."

"Should we?"

I wasn't even being a jerk. You might have noticed I'm good at avoiding conflict. I was giving him an out because I wanted one. But unfortunately he didn't take it.

"Look, it wasn't really great last time we saw each other. But it feels weird that we're not even on speaking terms. We were in a lot of each other's lives."

"It's... it's weird for me too," I said while walking through one of the park's gated exits. I held it open for him to follow. "I'm only going right over here. Why don't you sit down with me? How have you been?" I plopped down on a bench facing away from the courts and pulled water out of my bag.

Malik sat next to me and retrieved a bottle of some bright red sports drink. "I've been pretty good. I just graduated."

"Political science, right? What's next?" We both took a swig from our respective drinks before he responded.

"I've got some friends who can wedge me into a policy analyst job. I'd mostly be scoping out adjustments that can be made to make existing laws more beneficial. I'd be just starting out but I have a real passion for it. What about you? Last I saw you, you were working on a vet degree. Are you the Jane Goodall of puppies yet?"

I laughed. "No. I need more school and it's really expensive. So I've been doing some freelance accounting work to earn enough money to finish. It's actually been pretty interesting."

"That *is* interesting." He stared me down and I suddenly didn't know what he was thinking. "What brings you out to Pierce?"

Funny he should ask.

"Do you hear that?" In the distance, the sounds of police sirens grew louder and louder. Two patrol cars and two black SUVs with flashing lights came zooming in from both ends of the block. They skidded to a halt directly in front of where Malik and I sat. Indicative of where we were, a couple of ball players snatched up their stuff and took off through the far gate. The cops weren't there for them, though. Across the street from Pierce Park was the building that held both

Pierce High School and the administrative offices of the Cargill school district.

Malik got out of his seat and sat back down on the back of the bench. From his new heightened perch, he watched as the officers came pouring out of their cars and through the school's front door. The patrol cars had uniformed officers. The SUVs each carried multiple plainclothes detectives.

"Oh shit! That's Lifeline," he said from slightly above me. From one of the SUVs came a fat, beautiful Latinx woman. Her long hair swished as she moved, revealing the red cross emblazoned on the back of her jacket.

"She's a superhero?" I asked, although it was kind of obvious.

"Yeah, she's been helping to clean up this area. Her, King Corley, B-Girl, and a few others."

Hearing Camille's codename was a shock. I had no idea she was stationed here. I had just assumed she worked closer to my coffee shop. I didn't know anything about King Corley, but Lifeline looked like a twenty-something. B-Girl was old enough to have been a protector here back when I first started playing ball. If she was around making the place safer, I couldn't tell. The ballers that scattered when the police arrived told me that this place was pretty much the same as it was a decade ago.

"Who is that guy?" Malik said as Lifeline and one of the uniformed cops returned. Handcuffed in front of them was an older person in a tan jacket and horn-rimmed glasses. Lifeline restrained the prisoner in the back of one of the SUVs before going back inside. The other cop stayed outside to stand guard.

"That's Richard Caldwell, the treasurer for the school district for the last twenty-five years." I spoke without thinking.

"Wow!" Malik let out a low whistle. "Four cops, four detectives and a superhero for that pencil-pusher? I wonder what he did."

Again, I should've asked myself how much to reveal. Instead, I said, "That pencil-pusher has been handling the books for the district for decades. Unfortunately, that's included some pretty high-level embezzling of the district's budget. Damn near enough to build a whole new school."

Malik now glared. "That's foul. This school district has been under state intervention since we were kids. Imagine how much an area like Pierce could thrive if they weren't so damn underfunded all the time. All they do is make a dollar out of fifteen cents around here, and this guy was lining his pockets with money that could've gone to the kids who needed it the most? Y'know, this neighborhood hasn't always been shitty."

"Since when?" I scoffed.

"Part of the new job is knowing the history of the city, Ness. Sure, it's been bad here for the last twenty, twenty-five years. But before that, this was an area on the rise."

"Are you kidding? What happened?"

"That part is harder to say. It could be any number of factors. Bringing down an area is easier than it looks. You just add a few criminals here, a few parasites there, close a few businesses, and pay a handful of people to look the other way. Next thing you know, you've got a disenfranchised strip of land. All it takes is a pack of guys like this Richard Caldwell. That's exactly why I'm going into policy ana—" He

175

paused his rant, turned to me, then came down off the backrest to sit in a normal position. "Why are we sitting here, Vanessa? Did you know this was gonna happen?"

"Uh, yeah." I hung my head down. As eagerly as I explained the situation, I wasn't really prepared to have to explain myself. I just wanted to be here to see it happen. I wanted to make a change without getting shot at or having to navigate crime scenes. I didn't know I'd have an audience for this part. Fortunately, Malik didn't ask me any follow up questions. He didn't even seem surprised. But he was biting his lip. He always did that when he was deep in thought.

We sat quietly watching the detectives carry huge boxes of paperwork from the school to their car trunks. The news vans eventually arrived and Lifeline gave an interview that we couldn't hear from across the street. Even if she had spoken louder, the sounds of basketball behind us drowned out everything else. I was just thinking about going home to watch the news coverage when Malik looked at me and spoke again.

"You didn't know this was gonna happen. You made this happen. This is your freelance accounting job." It wasn't a question. I didn't give him an answer because he didn't need one. "It's awesome that you have this. It's better this way, you know. They'd have never let you keep playing."

I turned sharply. "What are you talking about?"

He spoke a little slower, more deliberately. "You being what you are. They'd never have let you go on to play pro ball. Maybe not even college."

"Fuck you, Malik." I rose to my feet. We'd had a rocky road, he and I, but I didn't expect this. Not from him. "The college game was integrated. The pro game was integrated. If the scouts had spotted me, I'd have gotten recruited to every school in the country. You know that! It wouldn't have mattered what I was assigned at birth. I was one of the best ballers in this damn city."

He jumped back in his seat, eyebrows creased. "I'm not talking about your gender, dummy." He waved his hands to acknowledge my body. "How could you think that? I'm talking about your... abilities." He looked around and whispered that last word as if the reporters across the street were listening in.

"My abilities?" I crossed my arms and leaned onto my back foot.

"You try to hide it. You pass it off as strategy and overthinking. But I watched your game film in high school. You're a point guard who averaged twelve boards a game our sophomore year."

"And twenty-five points and fourteen assists. So what?"

"I watched all of those rebounds and you were perfectly positioned for every single one." Shit. I knew where he was going with this. "You were ahead of every play before it developed. A brick would go up and you'd be moving to where the rebound would land before the shot even hit the top of its arc. You were always a step ahead of everyone on the court. It wasn't just court vision, *I've* got court vision! This was something else. And if I could spot it, someone who didn't want you to succeed could've spotted it too. Then they'd have taken the game away from you as sure as those missing scouts did."

He was right. Variants weren't allowed in competitive sports with non-variants, although that was usually applied to variants with

177

enhanced strength or speed. I never even thought of my enhanced perception as part of my game. Everything came to me naturally in a way that it didn't for everyone else. I always assumed it was a direct result of all the work I put in. And all this time I'd been bitter about how the game did me wrong, without ever pausing to consider how my variance might've factored in. But Malik noticed.

"I'm not judging. I'm proud of you. In high school you wanted to go pro. You wanted to be Dawn Taylor and that didn't work out. So, maybe, if you've got this, you can be a new Dawn playing a different game."

My jaw dropped. He'd had me pegged this whole time and never bothered to say anything. Instead, he'd kept quiet until right when I needed the validation the most. I sat back down next to him, rested my head on his shoulder, and reconsidered my stance on the existence of providence.

Vanessa Copeland: True Believer.

Chapter 30

Camille

OPERATOR ON THE RISE: A strong jump out of the gate for V-Girl, or Vanguard, or is it VanTage? Either way, clients should be on the lookout. After launching a career with four five-star operations, including two in one day, Operator #3683 is someone we expect to see on the power rankings before long.

Still Fighting After All These Years:

Celebrating For Hire*'s upcoming 30th anniversary seemed like a great time to look back at the heroes and operators that helped take us from a floundering hip-hop mag to the first and foremost source on superhuman culture. A good place to start would be in Cargill, N.J., home to the cream of the crop, Double M. Working out of the same department is an often-overlooked veteran from the days when* For Hire *was still called* Flow House*. Camille "B-Girl" Baston (she/her) can be filed under "classic." Her iconic costume hasn't changed much over the years from the street dancing styles of her youth. And while she's not about to* toss down a piece of cardboard and bust out a back spin, it's clear from her recent stops that she's still got the moves.

I visit her in her modest Cargill home. The decor is surprisingly minimalist for a woman who has been synonymous with 'bling' for as long as I've been alive. With her, as always, is her husband/manager, Reynolds Sterling-Baston. He's a big man, with a smile that lights up his face. He's your favorite uncle, flaws and all. They've been together since Camille came up in the meaner streets of Cargill, using her body control variance to round up the local toughs.

Interviewer: *For Hire* got started as rap magazine in 1988, but the famous power rankings didn't get started until 1997. A decade ago, to celebrate our twentieth anniversary, we went back in the archives, dug up every record we could find, and created a retrospective top ten ranking for each of those first nine years. Were you aware of that?

B-Girl: Yeah, I remember when the magazine did that.

Interviewer: Then you might know where I'm going with this. That ranking had you at number seven back in 1990. The seventh best hero in the country for the whole year. After that, you never rose higher than 18th and you haven't been in the Top 50 since before the turn of the century. What happened in 1990 and what's happened since?

B-Girl: '90 was the year. Hip-hop was at a high point. There were a lot of movies and TV shows that showed off the culture and B-Girl was on the rise. I married my second husband that year, Rey being my first. I had learned the ropes and I was really comfortable in the area I was protecting. I did some of my best work back then. After that, I got held back by the system.

See, part of being a superhero is being friendly to the right people. Even you right now. If I curse you out during this interview, you can make me look like trash in a magazine that everybody reads. That would damage my image and my career. I've never really been all that image-conscious and that's rubbed a lot of influential people the wrong way. So I didn't always get the advancement opportunities that other heroes got.

Interviewer: So what's kept you going all this time?

B-Girl: The feeling I've been doing the right thing.

Interviewer: With all the changes that have occurred over the course of your career, do you feel like you can still discern right and wrong properly at your age?*

B-Girl: That's kind of a bummy question. A hero without a strong sense of right and wrong is just a menace. Or an operator. A lot of standards change as people get older. Identities get discovered or highlighted. Terminology moves around. But right and wrong stay the same. There's no age where a guy robbing a bank stops being a guy robbing a bank. When I was eighteen in Hawkins, I'd punch that guy in the face and return the money. At fifty, in Cargill, I'd do the same thing.

Interviewer: You've had a recent resurgence in popularity. What would you attribute that to?

B-Girl: Like I alluded to before, part of the game is getting help from your support team. If you land on the wrong shift or get on the bad side of your dispatcher, they may take your opportunities away. I've had chances to make big stops given to other superheroes even though I was ready, willing, and available. My work was never bad. It was just consistently overlooked. So, when I started seeing ways to put *myself* in positions to succeed, I bet on myself and won big.

Interviewer: From what you're saying, wouldn't that rub some people the wrong way?

B-Girl: You know what the difference is between being seen as a trendsetting nonconformist and an insubordinate rebel? Politics. When you're cheerful and friendly, that maverick style of heroing will bump you up the ladder. When you're not-so-cheerful and not-so-friendly, it'll keep you buried at the bottom of the pile. I've chosen not to play ball but also not allow myself to get left off the field.

Interviewer: You've got about a decade left until you hit the mandatory retirement age of sixty. Do you have any goals you'd like to achieve between now and then? Do you even plan to stick it out another ten years?

B-Girl: Those people I rescued from the traffickers? Seeing what they went through makes me want to do a little bit more surrounding the conditions at play. I don't usually lean on the lawmakers, but it's never too late to start. Plus, I don't need to be active duty for that. So who knows when I'll wrap up my career? Right now, I'm riding a wave and it's good. I don't need to be brought back to shore just yet.

Something that gets obscured while fighting to meet deadlines is our tendency to become prisoners of the moment. Flashy young superheroes like Double M, Navarra, and La Realeza may capture our adoration in big bombastic ways. But veteran heroes like B-Girl still fill out rosters in every major city. Some act as mentors to the next generation and others are just chugging along. Either way, they deserve more attention than the public gives them. On that note, For Hire is glad to put the spotlight on one of Cargill's finest.

Ashlei Perry (she/they) is a writer out of New York City. Her areas of interest—other than superheroes—include anime, board games, and polyamorous novels.

*For Hire apologizes for the inherent ageism of this question and has left it in for transparency's sake.

Chapter 31

Vanessa

Black tank top and blue jeans, leather jacket, and my worn, comfortable boots—everything I needed to look completely not-nervous about this first date. Underneath, I wore my best matching bra and panty set. I doubted Bobby was going to see them, but being prepared didn't hurt. Plus, my cleavage looked especially good. Into it.

Was it too hot for the jacket though? We were having residual spring weather but I couldn't count on the night cooling enough. I reached for my phone to check the weather and saw that a call was coming in. Really? I had left the phone on vibrate on date night? Okay, fine, I was a little nervous.

The screen read C. Baston and displayed a screen capture I took of B-Girl's interview after the job at the docks. I hated to derail my date prep, but I hadn't heard from her in so long I didn't want to wait another month for her to remember I existed.

"Hey Camille! It's been a while. How are you?" I kept my tone even. I had a lot I wanted to say, but I didn't want to turn the conversation sour if I could avoid it.

"I'm good, thanks. I got something lined up for us. You ready to get this money?" It stung a bit that she didn't ask me how I'd been.

"Let's do it," I said, pushing my feelings aside. "When were you thinking?"

"Tonight. Rey can swing by and we can get it crackin'."

I flinched. "Tonight? That's kinda short notice for me, Camille." Not to mention that we hadn't done any scouting or prep work, but that was beside the point. "Can we do it another night?"

She went from zero to crabby instantly. "No, we can't do it another night! What you gotta do that's so important that you can't get this money with me?"

I paused, considering my options, but honesty seemed the best way to go. "I—I met a guy. It's our first date."

She made a dismissive noise. "Well, cancel that shit."

"It's in less than an hour! I just got dressed. I really like him. And his dog. If I cancel our first date he'll think I'm flaky."

"Oh I see," she said, her voice flat and annoyed. "You about to get some booty and you suddenly too good to do work? You said you needed this to be a regular thing, but now you're okay slinging coffee for the rest of your life." She made it sound like a death sentence. Did she forget I took pride in that work?

"I have a life, Camille. I need more than an hour's notice. Besides, I'm not a barista anymore." Not exactly true, but I was reacting without thinking now, matching her annoyance.

"Since when?" Ugh! Follow-up questions. I had planned to call out sick tomorrow if the date went well and then give notice over the weekend. I couldn't tell B-Girl that, though.

185

"I just put in my notice. I took a contract last week and it went really well, so well that I think I could be a full-time operator at least until—"

"Oooooh! So you're *really* too good then. You been doing work without me?" Steel-voiced. Kinda scary.

"I hadn't heard from you in weeks, Camille! Did you think I was just staring at my phone, waiting for you to call? I mean, I've seen the news, you've been doing work without me too." In the time since the Axion job, I'd seen reports of B-Girl taking down a series of drug labs. Small jobs individually, but massive when taken collectively. Same as with our joint work, there was lots of praise and photo opportunities to go around. Part of me felt ashamed that I didn't assume she was doing good work simply for the sake of doing good work. But I also had to wonder who was counting the money for her, if not me.

"I'm the superhero and you're the sidekick, Vanessa," she told me. "Any solo work I do is none of your business."

You know who else can go from zero to crabby fast? "I'm not a sidekick. I'm a partner, remember? And why are you angry? I thought you'd be proud of me, the way that I'm proud of you. You're getting everything you wanted. You took in more than a quarter million dollars from the places we hit together. Your profile is through the roof and I read your feature in *For Hire*, it was fantastic. We can do the job, B. Just not tonight."

"It's only available tonight. You're being real ungrateful right now. If it wasn't for me, you'd still be fixing drinks. My drinks. And now you think you're better without me?"

"Well, if it wasn't for me, you'd still be a nobody doing street-level busts for pennies!"

In case I needed it hammered home that I'd gone too far, Camille hung up without another word. I tossed my phone on my bed and stomped into the bathroom to do my make-up.

I was still a little edgy when, forty minutes later, I inhaled a turkey and provolone sub and dealt with the first date interrogation. Fortunately, the feeling was fading fast.

"So, are you seeing anyone?" Bobby asked. He was looking that same clean-cut way and I was there for it. Stephen sat patiently next to him, looking up in adoration. I wanted to do the same thing. His hug hello was just right.

"I'm seeing you. Right now, in fact," I said, grinning. He lifted his eyebrows at me, and I giggled and shrugged. "I'm sorta single at the moment. I was seeing a couple people for a while, but it was all very casual. Nothing's gonna play out well in the long run, so why get too invested?"

He was quiet for a few seconds. "How will it play out?"

"Well, I was seeing this one woman. She's great. She owns a collie named Gizmo—best name, right? She could afford fancy sandwiches and I couldn't which I guess makes her the... breadwinner?" Bobby rolled his eyes, but with a grin. "But seriously, she was really career-oriented, and I'm a barista." I thought about editing that last bit, but as I hadn't actually quit yet....

"Was she that superficial?"

I shook my head furiously. "No, no, I'm explaining it badly. It's like, between her success and my mediocrity, there'd be eventual tension, and one of us would break. Probably me." I looked at him. His expression hadn't changed, but I knew I'd said it wrong again. "Believe me on this. Casual is what works."

"Do you think they'd all play out like that?" I couldn't tell what he was probing for, but there was no judgment in the ask. He wasn't scared. He just wanted to know me.

"Nah. It's not about my ego or theirs, really. Adam wanted kids. Rashmi was living off a trust fund and it was that power imbalance again. Malik still had a playing career in college. Eventually, they'd all give me more than I could give back. Better to keep it chill or else cut it off entirely."

"So..." he said, smiling at me. "You're a variant. You see patterns. Kind of like rational precognition." I tried not to panic. "You're not guessing about how things will end. You're *seeing* how they'll end." He paused to take a bite of his meatball sub and washed it down with some concoction of three different soft drinks combined. It was only a few seconds, but I could feel my body tense up in preparation for the impending rejection. "My dad's like you—not a variant, but he sees patterns too. He's always taking notes, making charts, using whiteboards. Tracking trends is how he gets along. It's something I learned from him. I got curious when you mentioned the seafood, actually. Thanks for that tip, by the way." He leaned forward and took my hand. His skin was so soft for the son of a construction worker.

"I'm honestly amazed by abilities like yours, Vanessa. I'd love to be able to see it all without writing everything down first. I can see why it's a challenge, though. There have been times when my dad saw the writing on the wall and made decisions that not everyone could understand."

I didn't talk about my variance with anyone if I could help it, so this was a strange situation for me to be in, especially after my last hang with Malik. I didn't know how much to say or what to hold back. We didn't have the years of trust to build from that Malik and I had.

"You don't have to talk about it if you don't want," he said, searching my expression. His tone lightened and he looked down at his super-cute dog. "I don't like to talk too much about why I need Stephen, but I don't want you to feel like the only person who's being vulnerable here. I have epilepsy. Stephen is trained to look for signs of oncoming seizures and get help if I do start seizing. Is that—is that okay?"

"Yeah, of course," I said, startled. "Why wouldn't it be?" He lifted a shoulder in the most casual shrug I'd ever seen in my life. It was so casual as to indicate real hurt.

"For some people, it's not. Past partners. My dad."

"Your dad is mad at you for something you can't control?" My dad was a lot of things but he'd never come down on me for who I was. He might struggle with it, but he'd never get negative.

"My dad gets mad at *everything* he can't control. My epilepsy. My pansexuality." He laughed. Again, too casual to be real. "If it were up to him, I'd already have three kids and more coming. You know? To make up for him only having the one. But I don't know if kids are in my future. Maybe they are, but they'll be adopted. Maybe they aren't. Maybe, like him, I just don't have it in me."

I felt a protective feeling rise up in me. "I think the worst thing a parent can do is not love you for who you are. I know I'm lucky. My dad fucks up, but he's trying."

"My dad tries too, in his way. He fails a lot. He hates failure. But that's okay. I'm trying to teach him a different way. For what it's worth."

The pause made me think it was time to shift topics. "So what does a Development Manager do?"

He shrugged with a little smile. "It's just an excuse for my dad to give me a paycheck. Most days I don't do much of anything." I took in his slacks and button-down shirt. No sign of expensive designers. Even his shoes were mid-range.

"You don't dress like a trust fund kid," I teased.

"I spend my money on other endeavors," he said smoothly. "I'm more interested in building a better future than I am in buying name brands."

He then changed the subject to my interests, and I talked longer about basketball and video games than could ever be considered attractive. But his smile didn't falter, and I felt... pretty. Wanted.

I liked it.

Chapter 32

Camille

"What are you gonna do?" Rey asked from the front seat of the SUV. It had been twenty minutes since they pulled up to the location of the next bust. Since then, they sat in silence pondering the next move.

"Don't say anything, Rey. I need to think."

How could Vanessa have done this to her? Camille had gone out of her way to make all this possible, *for her*, only for that ungrateful brat to throw it back in her face. Hurt her feelings, even. She raised her hands to her head and massaged her temples. A moment later, Rey's hand reached back with her migraine meds, which she took with her right hand and swallowed dry. She couldn't risk getting even more distracted.

She stared at the burner phone in her left hand and fiddled with it until she pulled up the single saved voicemail message. She should've deleted it after memorizing the information, but just like the previous messages connecting her to her last several busts, she kept it stored until after the job was complete. Unlike those messages, Camille had listened to this one several times. She listened to it once more.

B. This one's for you and the kid. We've got a small group of growers who have gotten a bit full of themselves lately. Their work ethic and product quality have gone down drastically. So, they're done. Tonight.

I've just overpaid them for their latest haul. Your pup will be able to pick up on the overage, which you'll pocket. If we wait until the end of the week, they'll probably detect the surplus themselves and either pay it back or spend it. Either way, we can't pull this trick with them twice.

They've got exclusive ties to us. Hitting them will make it clear that B-Girl is hitting us too, when in actuality you're helping us take out the trash. That's another camera-ready bust for you, and the kid gets to feel useful netting another payday for you both.

It's only four guys. The big one has a military background but the rest are a bunch of nerdy stoners. 9760 Mason Street. 9pm.

The job itself was pretty uncomplicated. Since the Axion, B-Girl had shut down several drug labs at Teresa's request and everything had gone smoothly. Teresa's straightforward jobs had included a straightforward payday, delivered in cash directly to Rey's SUV at a drop-point both she and Teresa designated after the job was well done.

This time, the payday was inside with the job itself and required Vanessa's number skills to retrieve it. Camille should've just cancelled when Vanessa bailed. But she hated leaving money on the table and she didn't want to sour this business relationship by leaving things undone.

Blackwell had given her a time and a place. Now it was in her hands.

She tossed the burner to her husband and slipped on a small backpack that fit tightly against her back. After cinching the straps, she grabbed a leather belt with two black fighting knives slung in hip holsters from the seat next to her. She secured the belt without losing her stride as she stepped out of the back of the car and walked up to the three-story brick building. They were on the edge of the warehouse district late on a Thursday night. Nobody would hear a commotion out here as long as it didn't include much gunfire.

The only lights on were on the building's top floor. Colorful flashes indicated that a television was on too: a distraction. If all went perfectly, she would catch them completely unaware.

It was ridiculous, but Camille felt strange without the kid there, like something was missing. *A lot of babble and bad jokes*, she told herself. *That's what's missing. I'll get over it.* She wasn't thrilled with being the one literally carrying the bag, either. It messed up the lines of her jumpsuit. She ran her fingers through her hair, then took out a lockpick and began working on the front door. This would be the most difficult part. She had no idea what would be meeting her on the other side of that door.

What she found was nothing. With the door unlocked, she entered the darkened building to find an empty vestibule with a wide-open security gate and the stairway to the upper floors.

You're kidding me. This is the most unprofessional shit ever. Moving slowly, she pushed the cage door wide enough to slip through and listened for a reaction. Again, nothing. Even still, she drew a blade out in each hand and stalked silently from room to room. Camille was naturally adept at moving quietly, but still she slinked with deliberate concentration through the house.

The first floor consisted of a kitchen, a bathroom, a common area, and no criminals. The second floor appeared to be the work area. Every room contained tall plants, bagged shipments of bud, or stacks of cash. While B-Girl wasn't entirely familiar with the finer details of drug processing, she knew what half-finished work looked like. She understood why this team needed to be benched. Teresa had hinted at there being a place in her organization for Camille after she took over. If shutting down sloppy operations like this one was part of her responsibilities, she liked her future prospects.

Laughter and music from the third floor gave away her targets. If she were a thief, she could've just pocketed the money and drugs strewn around the second floor and left through the open security cage. She paused to consider it. But she wasn't just here for money, she wanted that shine too. High-profile careers weren't built on surreptitious nighttime theft—they were built on the spotlights and news cameras that showed up after you walked in and busted everyone you found there.

With that in mind, Camille crept up to the third floor. The flickering light she'd seen from the street was coming from the single door left ajar at the top of the stairs. Peeking through the crack, she took in the layout.

This attic was the party room. It was full of couches and had Christmas lights strung across the ceiling's perimeter, reminding her of back in the day with Rey. Cheesy pop music played lightly enough for conversations to be heard amongst the group: six people, likely the four

Teresa had mentioned and two femmes, maybe girlfriends and possible leverage. All were staring at a video game being played on a massive television mounted to a stretch of wall separating two large windows. The big one had his back to the door, a femme on his lap, and a gun sitting on a table between empty beer bottles. *These guys are pathetic. Might as well end their night.*

"Evening, everybody," Camille said in a strident voice as she pushed open the door and brandished the knives. She could only imagine how strange it looked to them as she held the blades out like one might level a gun at their enemies.

"You're B-Girl, right? I saw you on the news," a shaggy-haired boy said while carefully placing down a game controller. As Camille turned her head to address him, she used the reflection in the windows to follow the movements of the big man. His friend was very slowly sliding off his lap, trying not to draw attention.

"It's true. I'm B-Girl and the big guy is about to do something real silly. I wouldn't if I were you."

The grower with the shaggy hair gave an almost imperceptible shake of his head to the man across from him. It wasn't enough. The man lunged towards the coffee table and B-Girl flicked her wrist. The magnetic burst from her gloves pushed the blade to superhuman speed until it lodged in the wooden coffee table. Unfortunately for the big guy, it met his outstretched hand first.

A few screams rang out around the room, including from the pinned man himself. The person who had been sitting on his lap called to him in horror, "Greg!"

"Greg? I hear you're the man to worry about. Here's the deal, Greg." With her free hand, Camille loosened the top of the backpack, reached in, and tossed its contents to the closest stoner. "Your friends are going to use the zip ties in this bag to tie their wrists together. You're gonna go last. If any of them try to get cute, my other knife goes in your eyeball. Let's get started."

Camille picked up and dismantled the gun as the group quietly bound themselves. They were taking it surprisingly well. Except Greg, of course.

"Okay, kids, I'm going to go take one last look around while my friends on the force show up. I wouldn't move if I were you, Greg. That knife's the only thing keeping you from bleeding out."

Camille pulled her personal phone from inside the bag and called in the bust as she went downstairs to where the money was kept, closing the attic door behind her so she'd hear if they were foolish enough to try to escape. She saw the books, but the numbers meant nothing to her, and she didn't have the time to do the math anyway. The money was all out for the taking, but how much to take? Without the kid, she didn't have a clue. So she'd keep it low.

Fifty thousand was a pittance compared to the takes she'd been getting, but it seemed safe. Twenty-five thousand apiece for what would've been both of them—that sounded like what Blackwell would choose, to save herself a few bucks compared to Camille solo but still impress the kid. She tossed the money in the emptied backpack and tightened it as she heard the first sirens approaching. She would walk out to meet them and drop the bag where Rey could grab it.

As she passed through the front door, she made sure the non-powered cops heard her say, "Hey baby. I made a little bust around the corner of Mason and Wells. I might be a little late getting home..."

Chapter 33

Vanessa

The weirdest part was when JoMo himself tried to hug me goodbye. He was totally sincere, too, despite all the verbal abuse. He didn't even try to talk me into working an extra week on top of my two weeks' notice.

I biked home from my last day at JoMo's in rush-hour traffic, but nothing could bring me down. The previous phase of my life was ending and the next had already begun. I lived in the thrill of the overlap, where things felt both complete and new. Malik had texted about getting together to play ball over the weekend. I had at least five emails sitting in my account, all with offers on local jobs.

I had another date with Bobby set up for next week, too. I'd picked up extra shifts to accommodate Corey and Alma having to take up my slack until Joey could hire someone else, and Bobby was busy at work—"for once," he'd joked—but he was still finding time to message me here and there; sometimes flirty, sometimes supportive, sometimes just "thinking of you." I was giddy.

I'd even done the math and set a reasonable budget for getting back in school and having my own place. I was starting to feel optimistic about how the numbers were lining up against the rental market and trends in tuition costs. A few more jobs and those numbers would go from "optimistic" to "doable" and then to "absolutely comfortable."

Now I needed to tell my dad.

I'd been so busy with JoMo's during the day with operator work and social life (and sometimes more JoMo's) at night that I hadn't seen him much. Or I was avoiding him, whatever. After New York eliminated the Gizmos in the conference finals, our bonding time had dropped to nothing. I told myself it was something he had to get used to—empty nest and all—but I knew I was fooling myself. I got my bike situated and womaned up.

"Van?"

"Yeah, Dad. I'm home."

"Want some popcorn?"

"How about a real dinner, Dad?"

"What's that?" he joked, entering the room.

"Seriously, let's go out and celebrate my last day at JoMo's." His face fell, then immediately shifted to fake-neutral.

"You quit JoMo's?"

"I gave two weeks' notice. What about steaks?"

"Steaks, when you quit a job? This side gig must be paying well." He was still giving nothing away.

"It's doing great, Dad, and I wanna sit down and talk to you about it. Over steaks. Because steaks are delicious."

"Alright, Van." He got a light jacket in case the restaurant was cold and reminded me to bring a sweater. I run upstairs and quickly changed into a sundress. I grabbed a cardigan because, while he was usually wrong, this was the one thing he was always right about. Fifteen minutes later, we were shivering in a steakhouse. Shouldn't they be warmer?

"So tell me about the new job. I'm guessing that freelance work is going full-time?" he asked after we ordered drinks.

"Not exactly, but it's been lucrative. *Really* lucrative."

"I figured that out after the courtside seats," he said with a smile.

I flushed. "At least I didn't go out and buy everything I ever wanted?"

"Your restraint has been admirable," he said in a mock-serious voice.

"Seriously, Dad. It's good money. And it's been more stable than I expected. I'm getting a reputation as a—well, pretty much a forensic accountant."

His eyes widened. "That sounds..."

"Impressive? Rewarding? Yeah. I'm proud of what I've been doing and I want to continue doing it, but I also want to go back to school. And... I want to live on my own."

He paused, taking it in. "That's a lot, Van."

"Yeah, but I'm good for the numbers. You *know* I am. I wouldn't be talking about this if the numbers didn't add up."

He gave a little laugh at the pun and thanked the server placing our drinks on the table. "It seems like you've got it all in hand," he said.

"I'm not going to screw this up."

"I never said you would." *You didn't have to.*

"So...you'll help me move?"

"You mean this lucrative new job doesn't allow you to hire movers and save your old dad's back?"

Dad's practicality and doofy humor got us through the rest of the delicious dinner. We talked about apartments, and hidden expenses, and the little things I could say about the jobs I'd done. When we left the restaurant, it seemed like we both felt good about how it had gone. I was sure I did.

I immediately wanted to message Bobby and tell him about it. I had already started composing the text when I realized what I was doing. I looked at the words on the screen—"Had dinner with Dad. Told him I was moving out. It went well!"—and realized that for the first time in a long time, I was reaching out first. I hadn't really done so with him before, and I certainly had never done it with Elise. What was it about him that I liked so much? Or was I overthinking it?

When I got home, I hadn't heard back from Bobby yet, but that was normal lately. He hadn't gotten done work until after nine every night this week so far. As I got ready for an exciting night of gaming with my nerd pod, I sorted emails while waiting for my buddies to sign in. There were two jobs I could do next week, now that my days weren't taken up by JoMo's. Prepping for an audit of a local animal shelter? Embezzler at the largest nonprofit after-school program in Cargill? VanGuard, or whoever, to the rescue!

When I thought about the possibility of another *For Hire* mention, though, it reminded me of Camille and how badly we left

201

things. B-Girl being B-Girl, there was no way she was going to reach out first, so it had to be me. I wasn't happy about it, but sucking it up a little was better than not knowing where we stood.

Plus, you know, she could kill me with her hair. It was probably best to stay on her good side.

Chapter 34

Camille

"You wanted to see me, boss?" Camille walked into the captain's office to find her sitting at her desk watching a television mounted in the room's far corner. The volume was muted, but on the screen Camille could see a stage surrounded by what appeared to be an excited crowd. The camera turned to focus on the famous magician The Amazing Magisteria, who was hovering over the audience while sitting on a cloud of smoke and fire.

"Close the door and sit down." Double M paused the video feed, wiped her face with the back of her hand, and scooted her chair closer to the desk. Her eyes were puffy. "I thought we were buds, Baston. I thought we were BFFs. We had a deal." She sniffled.

Camille was fascinated by any turn of events involving the Captain looking like a mess but still couldn't keep the annoyed look off her face. "I never made a deal with you."

"That's right. I held out my hand and you left me hanging. 'My busts are clean, Captain' or whatever you said." She pulled a red folder from a stack in front of her. "Do you still stand by that?"

Camille rolled her eyes but didn't answer. She wasn't going to give Double M the satisfaction of watching her incriminate herself.

"No, I didn't think you would. You see, criminals, in general, aren't always the best at math. You've been around long enough to know that when their books don't balance, they usually report less money than they really have on hand. It's typically a matter of incomplete record-keeping. No big deal. Those times when the written count is higher than the paper bills, though, is because someone is stealing." Double M opened the red folder and pulled out a sheet of paper. She turned it to face Camille and slid it across the desk. It was an itemized list of seized property.

"According to this, that grow operation you shut down was roughly thirty thousand dollars short of the cash they say they had. These are internal numbers. Unless those four chuckleheads in lockup were ripping themselves off... you know where I'm going here."

Camille let the accusation hang in the air. "What do you want from me here?" she asked finally, her voice tight.

"I thought I made myself clear the last time we had this talk. What I *want* is the time and space to be properly upset with my personal shit without having to wash your dirty laundry." Camille narrowed her eyes.

"Still having relationship problems?"

"Do you honestly give a fuck?" M's look of disbelief was skeptical with a side of mocking.

"About your problems? Not really. But if you're unraveling, I should have a good idea of how much so I can point to it later."

The captain let out a loud, long laugh she couldn't seem to control. It made Camille uncomfortable. When her laughter died down, she began wiping tears from her eyes again.

"There's my favorite self-centered superhero." Double M took a deep breath to regain her composure. "My relationship problems have gotten worse, actually, but if you think that's going to be leverage during an investigation, you're fooling yourself."

Camille watched M's eyes flicker to the screen. "You and The Amazing—"

"Stop." Double M put her hand up. "The details aren't important. Not to you, anyway. What's important is that shit rolls downhill. If the major and the chief are giving me shit for backing you, I've got to give you shit for being this difficult to back. So, how do I clean up a mess like B-Girl?"

"Why don't you just stop being cutesy and tell me what you need from me?" Camille's glare could cut like a dagger, but everything bounced off of Double M's fancy armor even when she wasn't wearing it.

"I need you to accept that your race is run," M told her. "It's either that or we get Internal Affairs involved in this mess and find out what else you fucked up. They'll likely call the I.R.S. and make sure you and Rey are living on a cop's salary. You two haven't paid off any huge debts or made any large purchases lately, have you?" She raised an eyebrow.

That smirking bitch.

"You smirking bitch! You think you can bully me with I.A.?"

M shrugged. "It's only bullying if your busts are a hundred percent clean. We both know they aren't. There was never a shortage of people who thought the worst of you, and I've been able to keep that limited to locker room chatter. But covering for your completely uncharacteristic resurgence was only easy while your work looked legit. I'm sure they were all dirty, but this latest bust actually *looks* dirty. So, covering for you isn't so easy for me anymore. To be honest, Camille, you should be grateful."

It was Camille's turn to laugh hysterically. "Grateful for what?"

"For how much time I've bought you."

"Yeah, but at the end you're still going to let I.A. destroy the little bit of a reputation I've even got. Oh, thank you *sooo* much for giving me just enough rope to hang myself with." Her anger rose and rose. The Captain was now cool as a cucumber.

"That's not what's happening here. Not if you play this right."

"Is this the part where you tell me to bend over?" Camille snapped.

"Camille, you're going out a hero. I don't mean that in a sarcastic or threatening way either. Your profile is higher than it's ever been. You had a trash legacy that you've almost entirely rebounded in the last six months. At least publicly, if not here in the office. Either way, you couldn't have asked for a better turnaround. So, now I need you to do the right thing." *For once*, the pause said. "Retire."

"Retire? Fuck you. I've got almost another decade before—"

"You've got until year's end to put your badge on my desk," Double M told her. "After that, we go a whole 'nother way. That gives you a few months to finalize whatever you've got going and to come up with a believable story for why you're getting out when you are. But this is it. You're done."

"So this is the deal you're offering?"

"Our deal expired. Now it's an ultimatum. On January 1st, it becomes a fight. I'm hoping you're smart enough to keep it from getting to that point. But then again, I was hoping you were smart enough to keep it from getting to *this* point, too."

"You—"

"Get the fuck out of my office, Camille." Her tone was even but the message was clear: the conversation was over.

And so was her career.

Chapter 35

Vanessa

The phone was ringing.

Had this been a romantic relationship, I would've ghosted by now. In hindsight, the logical closure point for Camille and I was somewhere between when I five-starred my first solo contract and when she hung up on me. It would've allowed me to avoid all this conflict and confrontation, which, to be honest, was the opposite of my strong suit. But I wasn't still so afraid of the future that I gained comfort in the idea of hiding from it. So, instead of ghosting, I called her. Surprisingly, she picked up.

"Hey, Camille."

"Hey." I couldn't read her tone of voice. I had to get her talking.

"The way we ended our last conversation? I didn't want to just leave it that way."

She paused. "Me neither. I missed you on that last job. I'm glad you called." I couldn't tell if it was me that she missed or the work, but at least she didn't sound mad anymore. "I'm sorry I got salty with you. Things have been a bit stressful over here and that's not your fault. How was your date?" Wow, asking about me for once. Hearing that really helped, actually.

"The date went great!" Thinking of Bobby made me blush all over again. "I felt really seen by the guy. There was a real connection, I think. I wasn't expecting to see him again so soon after our first date, but it's becoming a regular thing."

"That's sweet. I'm happy for you." Okay, I got my warm fuzzies. Time to move on.

"So, um, I saw that your work has really been taking off. How's that been going for you?"

"It's been alright, I guess. I've been considering hanging it up after this year. I can't be B-Girl forever, right? It may be time for the next chapter or whatnot."

"Does that mean we won't be working together anymore?" And just like that, I was really glad I made the call. A logical closure point presented itself without me having to force it. I couldn't have asked for more.

"Actually, I've got something popping tonight, if you've got the time. I don't want you to force it though if you've got another date."

Oh c'mon! Not fifteen seconds ago, the story of B-Girl and V-Girl ended with us walking off into the sunset, but in opposite directions (don't ask me why the sun was setting on both sides of the Earth). The smart thing to do would be to decline the offer.

"What kind of work is it?" I asked. Dammit! You didn't need further details to decline an offer. There was a part of me that was curious. Forensic accounting, if that's what we were going to keep calling it—and I think it legally was—was not the same as watching

Camille beat up the baddies. It was just one night of work. I could always end the partnership afterward.

"Word got back to me that a local arms dealer is biting the hand that feeds them. They're stiffing one of their major clients on an order, which means their pockets are heavier than they're supposed to be."

"And it's our job to make a change in the weather."

"I'm sorry?"

"It's about to be raining coins." She sighed, but with affection, I thought.

"I really don't know what to do with you."

What she ended up doing with me was sending me a contract for the night's bust. A B-list contract for freelance accounting with a fifty-percent split. I needed that partner split, since I wasn't one-hundred percent comfortable jumping directly into a new job a few hours after learning about it.

That's how we landed in front of a pawn shop in Pierce. I was reminded of my very first professional outing with Camille. Evidently, she was too.

"Unlike the casino, this building only deals out of the first floor. Word is, they've got a storeroom in the back with a pretty well-stocked arsenal, but we've got the element of surprise on our side. It'll be over for them before they even know it started. Then you can run in and do your thing." Instead of her baseball bat, I saw that B-Girl was strapping on a belt with a pair of knives. She noticed me watching her.

"There's only two guys in there, but they're definitely going to be better with guns than those casino guards. I doubt I'll need the blades, but if shit gets hot I'll want to end it quickly."

By "end it," she meant killing these guys. I took a deep breath and remembered how smoothly the casino job went. I was hoping for another night like that. I stepped out of the SUV and gave Rey a little wave.

As soon as it was possible to go wrong, it did.

Almost ten yards away from the storefront, we got made—twice! First, a pair of teenagers ran across the street to block our path. "Oh my god, are you B-Girl?" one of the teens asked.

"I love your work. You saved all those people on that boat. Can I have your autograph?" The two of them dug into their respective backpacks and budged in front of each other to produce something for Camille to sign. I was stuck. The plan was for me to follow her into the pawn shop. But if she stopped moving, I had to as well. At least she had a reason to pause. I was just randomly hovering twenty feet away trying to figure out how not to look suspicious. I hadn't quite come up with anything when an SUV pulled up in front of the building. A passenger hopped out holding a duffle bag. A delivery was being made, or at least it was until B-Girl and her two admirers were spotted.

It was impressive how quickly the thug assessed the situation. Wasting no motion, they turned back to the car mid-stride and opened the driver's side rear door. I couldn't hear what was being said to the driver, but the duffle bag was quickly tossed into the backseat. Tires screeched as the SUV peeled out and all hell broke loose when a yell announced "Yerrrrrrr, it's B-Girl!" The thug pulled out a gun and began firing at us.

I dove to the ground and immediately felt like it was the wrong move. Prone, I had no means to protect myself or fight back. Camille

211

pushed the two kids behind a parked car and spun around to engage the shooter. Bullets were still flying as the thug side-stepped towards the pawn shop. B-Girl was the target, but she was too fast to pin down. I remembered that she said she wasn't as good at dodging objects as she was with bodies. She was plenty good in that moment though.

The thug made one fatal error by looking away from their prey in order to reach for the store's door handle. The time it took them to grasp it was the same time it took for B-Girl to throw a knife in return. It was a direct hit right in the chest. The firing stopped and the body tumbled sideways into the entryway, where it blocked the door from closing. Something about the partially-open door shook me out of my fear long enough to get back on my feet.

At the same time, B-Girl turned to direct the two scared teenagers into a nearby alley. They almost knocked me over in their rush to safety. Had they, it might've meant my life, as the half-open door widened to produce a second shooter. This one was hiding behind a riot shield. B-Girl darted towards me and forced us both into the alley's protection.

Safety was short-lived, as this one was still firing and crept ever closer to our position. The teens were both screaming and I couldn't draw enough breath to do the same—I wanted to, but I couldn't. B-Girl, on the other hand, looked more annoyed than anything. Her back was pressed to the wall and she had her second blade out, flipping it almost casually in her right hand. She leaned out of the alley just enough to toss the knife in an overhand lob. Had it been a grenade, the throw would've made sense. There was no way she could've made an effective strike at a shielded oppo—

She clenched her fist and drew her hand back sharply. Again, the gunfire stopped, this time punctuated by a sharp grunt.

B-Girl glanced at me, winked, and strolled out of the alley. I couldn't believe it. I had to see. As I stepped out myself, I saw one of the shopkeepers face down on the sidewalk. B-Girl knelt down and dragged the riot shield from underneath the dead body. She fixed it to her right arm before kneeling again to pull her knife out from the back of the shooter's neck.

"Fucking magnets!" She laughed. Then she opened the storefront door and ran in with the shield held high. The sound of gunfire rang out again, but only briefly. A moment later, B-Girl walked back out holding both of her blades. Her dark red jumpsuit hid the stains as she wiped the knives clean on a sleeve and put them back in their holsters.

"You're up, kid."

I blinked. "I—I can't," I choked out. My hands wouldn't stop shaking. "I'm too scared. I can't focus. Even if I could, we don't have time. With all the gunfire, the police will be here soon."

"So what did we even do this for?"

"B-Girl! Those kids need medical attention." I pointed to the alley and suddenly winced in pain. A bullet had grazed my left arm so slightly it stung like a paper cut—a huge freakin' paper cut. "I need medical attention," I said through gritted teeth.

Camille called Rey and he showed up what felt like a moment later with a first aid kit. Rey was starting to grow on me. But that could've been the minor blood loss talking. I absolutely did not feel well. And by that I meant I was crying like a baby.

213

"I can't do this, B," I said between wails. "I can't."

She looked like a deer in the headlights. No, like someone had just handed her a newborn. And I was the newborn.

"Kid, sometimes it's tough," she said in a steady voice. I tried to match her breathing before I worked myself into my first operator-related panic attack. "Sometimes the job ain't pretty."

"I don't have powers like yours, Camille. I just want to look at ledgers and point people in the right direction. I didn't want to get *shot*."

"No one ever wants to get shot. But this is how we make the big bucks."

"I think I'd be okay with the medium bucks," I told her as I turned my face away and focused on my breathing. She got the hint and walked away to comfort the two fans. Rey took me by the hand, helped me up, and silently got me home.

When I finally could sleep, I had nightmare after nightmare.

Chapter 36

Camille

"Can I take your order?"

Camille was annoyed. These were the first words that had been spoken to her since she arrived, and she had been sitting in the same private booth across from Teresa Blackwell for more than five minutes.

"Bourbon. Double," Teresa spoke while finally looking up from her newspaper. She spared the slightest of glances at Camille while adding, "And whatever she's having."

"I'm good," Camille responded. She wasn't there to have a drink. There were bigger fish to fry.

"No. You're not," Teresa pressed, still looking down at the page. "Order a drink. This is gonna be one of those conversations where you'll wish you had." Camille relented.

"Rum and coke then."

"Make hers a double as well." The waiter ran off to fill the order. A few silent minutes later, he returned with the promised beverages. After the drinks were set down, Teresa pulled the curtains closed and set aside her paper. She lightly traced her fingers around the rim of her glass of bourbon before picking it up to take a sip.

"B-Girl saves the lives of two teenagers and brings down a pair of arms dealers. That's really good press."

That pause, though. "But?"

"It was a really sloppy play. The best part of your casino takedown is that the people at the top, myself included, didn't know it was happening until we saw it on the news. I asked you to take down a two-man operation. I didn't think it needed to be said, but it was supposed to be quiet."

"Quiet or loud, they're a problem you don't have to deal with anymore. Ain't that what you wanted?" Camille picked up her glass but didn't drink.

"You got rid of old problems while creating new ones. One of the arms dealers called my direct line for backup not long before you killed him. He's dead and it was a private call. I could safely ignore that. I couldn't ignore the delivery driver who showed up a few minutes later and loudly told all of us that B-Girl was ambushing the drop."

"Obviously that wasn't what I was doing, and why was a drop being made right at that moment anyway? I thought these guys were shorting you for pay. Why send them more money?"

Teresa's expression tightened. "That wasn't my call. Someone else authorized a new deal with them when you were already en route—and that's the problem. I'm in the middle of a power struggle and you're causing problems that require me to show force—force I can't possibly show because, unbeknownst to the rest of the crew, you're also a part of my plan. That other delivery boy, the one you shanked, he was well-liked. He was a good soldier with lots of potential and I can't even avenge him properly. Your compounded fuck-ups are making me look weak."

"What do you want me to do about it? I went where I was supposed to go and I did what I was supposed to do. *You* set this gig up."

"I set it up for you and your kid at *your* request. And the money I purposefully mismanaged? That's in a police lockup right now because your pup couldn't handle the pressure. So you bungled the hell out of a bust and didn't even get paid for your trouble. At least you got good press though." She said the last bit with a heavy dose of sarcasm.

"Is this what you called me about? Because I've got bigger problems to deal with. Double M is on my ass." Teresa's eyes widened.

"Meaning what? What does she know?"

"Chill. She don't know about you. She barely knows about me." Camille stifled a smirk. She had been on her heels for this whole conversation. It felt good to see Teresa flinch. She understood the reason, too. Nobody wanted to go head to head with the country's top hero. "All Double M's got is a hunch and count that was off from those growers you had me hit."

Teresa took another sip of her drink and let out a deep sigh. "Why was the count off? I thought the kid could handle the math."

"She wasn't there. She couldn't make it."

"What do you mean she couldn't make it? Keeping her in play was the whole point. I thought maybe when I took over the organization, we'd find a place where she could be useful." She paused for a moment, seeming to come to a decision. "Hear this the way I'm hearing this, Camille. All the work I've thrown you has gone smoothly with the exception of the ones involving this child. Maybe she's weak or maybe she makes you weak. Either way, she's sounding like a liability to me."

"Don't worry about her. Didn't you hear me say Double M is involved? She's forcing me to retire by the end of the year. We're not going to be able to do this much longer."

Teresa shook her head. "That's fine. That's actually the initial reason I called you here. A few snafus aside, I'm about ready to make my big play. The boss's health is getting dicier, which is to say, I'm about to *make* it dicier and I wanted to get your final decision on your continued involvement." The shift in conversation seemed to relax Teresa, and her softer tone made Camille feel less defensive than she had been. That didn't mean she was willing to let her guard down.

"I've made a lot of money working for you and working for myself," she said slowly, thoughtfully. "For the first time in decades, I got more money than I owe. Maybe I should just let this be the end."

"Congratulations, you're in the black. But how far in the black? I'm sure you've got a police-issued retirement fund, but outside of your debts, are we talking about walking-around money or Caribbean cruise money? Can you even spend all that off-book money you've made without tipping off the watchdogs?"

A fresh start away from a life of action was a beautiful dream, but Teresa was right. All of Camille's new cash was bundled in her basement. Spending big bucks now would only alert the wrong people that she had it.

"What are you offering?"

"Same as I said before. You've got a lot of useful knowledge and experience that can help me and my growing organization. In exchange for your services as a consultant, I'm offering a steady and lucrative paycheck and an easy path for money laundering. You've got to be sitting on more than a million by now. You can stay under the radar by spending it month-to-month for the rest of your life or I can help you spend it however you see fit. Right away, and far from Double M's watchful eye."

"A consultant. So no more fighting?"

"You know we're not in a safe business, Camille, but physical scrapes won't be part of your everyday job description either. We've stayed in the shadows for this long. We couldn't do that if we had people shooting up our city streets, this last occurrence notwithstanding."

"Okay. What do we need to do to make this happen then?"

"Well, first things first, we've got to discuss what we're doing about your pup."

Chapter 37

Vanessa

All he'd said was that he wanted to make up for all the work he'd been doing lately that had been keeping us apart. He never said we were going to a nice restaurant without Stephen. Or that he'd paid to keep it empty for the night. Or that a band would be playing just for us.

But there we were at Cammie's, a classy place as well-known for its Caribbean cuisine as for its live music. The emptiness of the restaurant had made me feel awkward at first, but as I settled in, it began to feel romantic: the soft light of the candles, the direct attention of the staff, the feel of Bobby's hand tight on mine in the middle of the small table that was never allowed to become cluttered, and the plaintive sounds of the soloist, a handsome Latinx trumpeter.

Afterward, the horn player came up and Bobby made an introduction as if they were old friends.

"Vanessa, this is Mateo Alvarez-Baston."

"It's lovely to meet you, Vanessa." I picked up only a slight lilt in their voice—maybe that of a local who grew up around accented speakers.

"That was amazing. You're amazing. Wait—Baston? Like Camille Baston?" Oh my god, I never made the connection: *Cammie's*. Mateo smiled.

"Of course, you've heard of Camille. She's seen a renaissance of late, yes? I'm her ex-husband. Do you mind if I sit down with you for a bit?"

"Join us," Bobby said before I could.

Mateo Alvarez-Baston slid out a chair and sat down. Every movement he made was graceful. In a way, it reminded me of B-Girl but without the precision. But after meeting Rey, Mateo was a big surprise.

"Mateo and I have worked together on a couple of fundraisers," Bobby said, smiling at me. "He's not only a talented musician, but also a humanitarian." Mateo blushed. I realized the older man was looking at Bobby in a fond way that was absolutely adorable. This man who could convert air into magic using only a piece of brass, who had been married to one of the strongest women I'd ever met, who was an 11 on a 1-to-10 scale, had a crush on Bobby!

"I do what I can, same as you, Bobby."

"Why did you and B-Girl break up?" The words came out of me even before I knew I needed to ask them. This was the part of Camille she didn't discuss, and I wanted access. Mateo's face dropped. "I'm so sorry. I didn't mean to pry. I just—"

"It's fine. Really." He closed his eyes and exhaled. "Camille and Rey and I fell in love young. You could say I was their unicorn, if the kids still use that phrase." He laughed a little, maybe at himself. "They were already together for their first anniversary at a jazz club where I was performing. I saw them, beautiful and glowing with love, and I wanted

221

to be a part of that energy. I found them both captivating. Rey was so strong, and so protective of both of us. It took me a while to realize that his choices, no matter how well-meant, always turned out the opposite of how he'd expected." He took a moment, remembering. "Camille was an up-and-coming superhero, full of energy and fire. It was a few years before I realized that she needed everyone else to feed that fire for her or else she'd smolder. They were star-struck when the money came in. None of us had grown up with much, so we spent recklessly at first, but then I pulled back and asked them to be a little more responsible, look to the long-term. They made promises they couldn't keep. There was a lot of impulsive spending. I'd make a budget and they'd laugh at me, and suddenly there'd be a new car.

"I could've handled the money issues. I ended up separating my finances, but Camille took it personally—the thing about Camille is that she *always* takes things personally. If someone bumps into her, it's because they hate her, that sort of thing, and it only got worse over the years. When *For Hire* blew up, and she kept getting overlooked, she got more and more miserable. She took a lot of that anger out on us. I didn't want to be in such a toxic environment. I asked her for a few things—therapy, a financial planner—and she refused. I asked her to think about early retirement, but she kept chasing bad guys and being upset that more fame didn't follow."

He looked at me, and the hunger he saw in my face was likely obvious, because he continued. "I wanted kids. The only kids she wanted were ones to follow her when she walked down the street. Meanwhile, Rey only wanted what she wanted. I couldn't even talk to him. He couldn't see my side at all. It was untenable, unfortunately, but it still took me so long to leave. I'd chosen not to tour after the first few years because of her neediness and disappointment. My career, while not derailed, had been... less because I put her first. I wanted to put myself first, my needs for once, but I knew she would only accept that if I left completely. One day, I finally did it. I packed up a few things while she was on patrol, left a letter, and stayed with a friend."

He looked so sad I wanted to reach out, but I didn't feel comfortable doing so with a stranger. Bobby gently placed an arm around Mateo's shoulders. I wondered if this was the first time he'd heard this story. I thought maybe it wasn't. While Mateo's words rang true, there was a flow to it that suggested it had been told many times before.

"She was livid, of course. She can't stand anything she thinks is a betrayal, and this was the biggest of all. She came to the club, made a scene—during operating hours, of course. When she realized she couldn't change my mind, she sent Rey to do it. I love him, but he's nothing but her puppet in some ways and her enabler in others. I sent him away too. She sent a lawyer next. I gave in to every demand. Everything but the restaurant.

"I do what I can for her. I know they haven't fixed the money situation, so I've been buying some of their art anonymously. It was mine too, I suppose, but like I said, she sent a lawyer, and I didn't want to argue anymore. I miss them all the time, but I know I made the right call."

"You did, friend," Bobby said softly, his lips near Mateo's ear as he rested his head against the side of Mateo's.

Mateo's shoulders rose with a deep breath. Bobby sat back in his chair, but his arm dropped to make slow, comforting circles along Mateo's back.

"What's done is done," Mateo said finally, then looked me right in the eyes. "Vanessa, I hope I haven't spoken too poorly of Camille. She and Rey were the loves of my life and though I stayed longer than I should have, I don't regret the attempts to make it work. She was in a hole, and she's never dealt with that well before." He stood. "I already feel I've said too much." As he turned to leave, his eyes were filled with unshed tears, and my heart broke for him. He put his career, his life, on hold for love, and while I wouldn't do the same, I sympathized with his story.

It was a lot to take in, and as he said goodbye I knew I sounded a little distant. I'd been seeing it all in my head: young Camille, like she was in her pictures, with her manager-husband and her artist-husband. Her power was unusual and afforded her the upper hand in many battles. But she did the barest of the work; I'd seen that now myself. She was sloppy with planning and relied on her powers for everything. She would never be famous like Double M. Double M knew how to market herself, and look at the bigger picture. B-Girl couldn't keep her eyes on the prize because she didn't know what that prize was really supposed to be. In my opinion, the prize should have been the good works, and the fame a result of that, not the prize itself. B-Girl was an actress in D-list movies wondering why she hadn't won an Academy Award. She was on the bench wondering why she wasn't the MVP.

And I'd almost tied my future to hers.

As sad as her story was, and even though I was now another person who wanted better for her, it wasn't my story and I couldn't act like it anymore, no matter how much I wanted her approval.

The charged emotions in the room dimmed down a bit as the band went back to playing a slow tune at Mateo's signal. Bobby signed for the bill and we walked out to the parking lot. Immediately everything I was thinking came bubbling to the surface.

"What was that, Bobby? What is this, this date? That restaurant? Meeting B-Girl's ex-husband? You can't tell me that was a coincidence." Bobby guided me to his car by barely touching the small of my back, and my stuffed brain was momentarily distracted by his fingers.

"You're right," he said in a calm voice, meant to soothe but not placate. "It wasn't a coincidence. After what you texted me the other night, I knew this was a connection you needed to make."

It wasn't like I glowed when my powers worked or anything, but I had to agree with him, if reluctantly. The more information I had on Camille—even biased info—the easier it was to see her patterns of behavior. I guess he took my silence as agreement because he kept talking.

"I didn't think you'd believe me if I just told you."

"Told me what?"

"B-Girl is going to kill you." I stopped next to the passenger door of his fancy-but-not-too-fancy car.

"Stop it," I said. "That's not funny." He looked at me from over the low roof, his expression more serious than I'd ever seen it.

"I'm not joking. I'm worried for your life, Vanessa."

"I don't know what you're talking about."

"Yes, you do. You're an operator and B-Girl is your client. You practically said as much the other night. I filled in the blanks," he said in response to my dropped jaw. All I had said was that I'd been working when there was gunfire. I supposed seeing me and B-Girl in the same place the night we met plus a little internet search for where shots were fired when I'd texted had gotten him there. I was impressed.

"Okay. Okay." I was talking more to myself than him, calming myself down, giving myself space to think. "But even if that was true—and I'm not saying it is—how does that lead to B-Girl wanting to kill me? Or do you mean she's going to get me killed?" He looked around and saw no one in the parking lot but still came around to my side of the car, dropping his voice.

"Either B-Girl is about to call you for a job or she already has. That job isn't hitting some random crime spot. It's hitting my father. Robert Senior. He's the big score."

I blinked. Of all the things I thought Bobby might say, this wasn't anywhere near the list.

"What? How? He's a construction guy."

"He's also a mobster. All of his legal businesses and charitable works are fronts for the city's largest crime enterprise."

I searched his face to find the joke, but I wasn't finding it anywhere. He was serious. His dad's money was at least somewhat dirty. I'd never had enough information to make the connection, but it explained why he was at the scene of our second job despite the place being seemingly closed. The shark-eyed woman from the bar, Teresa, worked for Robert Quinn, Sr. But....

"What you're saying doesn't make sense, Bobby. What me and B-Girl have been doing are small busts. Individual locations." I abandoned the idea of hiding the truth from him. He would see through it anyway, and I didn't want him to think that his confiding in me didn't mean something to me that I'd figure out later. "There's no way we can hit the largest crime enterprise in the city. Even with B-Girl's abilities, it's unbelievable."

"It's unbelievable if you want to take it *down*, yeah. It's completely believable if you want to take it over." He took in my widened eyes and seemed reassured by my reaction, because he gave a small nod. "You don't have to damage the structure at all to kill and replace a leader. My dad has been untouchable for decades. The cops can't get to him. The superheroes can't either. But Teresa Blackwell can, with B-Girl's help."

"But if she takes over your dad's organization, where does that leave you?"

"Right next to you... in a shallow grave as the only two loose ends of a mostly bloodless coup." We stared at each other for a while. I let all the new information get sorted by my variance.

"Why aren't you just telling your dad about this? He could just have Teresa killed or something." And now I was condoning murder. Great.

"You think he'd listen to me? You think he'd believe me? Blackwell has been with him longer than I can remember. He trusts her more than he's ever trusted me."

227

"This is ridiculous! You're not a mobster. You sit in an office all day and listen to people complain about being mad at their co-workers. Why would anyone think you're a threat?"

"My last name makes me a threat. Yeah, most people see my service dog and write me off as weak, but some people really believe in family and legacy. Even as a figurehead, I'm worth something."

"You really think Blackwell wants you dead?"

"I do. When he doesn't need her for dirty work, my dad uses her as a bodyguard for me, and I've heard her say more than once that she's sick of 'babysitting.' She's never shown one sign of seeing me as a real person, and I think that resentment and her need for power is going to keep her from ever doing so."

He covered his face with his hands and then dropped them with a sigh. "When I was younger, I thought of her as my avenging angel. My father's enemies have tried to kill me over the years, but I'm pretty sure she's not going to stop the next one. I don't want both of us being murdered by the two people who are supposed to have our respective backs." I was jolted out of my sympathy.

"Don't say that. B-Girl wouldn't hurt me."

He shook his head, looking annoyed for the first time in the conversation. "You've been around her long enough to know what kind of person she is. Tell me it's out of character for her to burn bridges in extreme ways. Tell me she wouldn't form an unexpected alliance if it improved her situation—like, say, with an inexperienced variant barista who can help her skim money from criminals."

"That's different. That's not illegal. That helps the greater good. B-Girl is a hero."

228

"A superhero hiring an operator to tamper with and steal crime scene evidence *is* illegal, for her anyway. Nobody would care because it's drug and gun money, but ethics and legality aren't really what B-Girl's career is made of. Even if all she wanted was fame, she could've spent the last thirty years cleaning up crime spots the exact way she has been lately. But instead she waited until she could turn a profit from it."

"So she's selfish and flawed. That doesn't make her a murderer."

He took my hand and, like a fool, I let him. "When you told me that you'd been shot, I wondered if it was a set-up. Can you honestly tell me that's not possible?"

I didn't speak.

"Look, cards on the table. I've bribed some of Blackwell's men and they told me the hit is going to happen soon. What does B-Girl need an accountant for on a hit? If she calls you, call me. I can protect you. Please, Vanessa. I don't want anything to happen to you."

I took my hand away. "This is all too much. I—I don't believe this. I don't believe you. I want to go home." He opened the car door and I got in. The silence in the car was overwhelming. My head was spinning from all the new information and possibilities.

Camille Baston was a lot of things, but was she the kind of person who could kill her own partner for money and power?

Chapter 38

Camille

Hey, kid. Making sure you're alright.

Call me back, Ness. We've got work to do.

I'm sorry, okay? I fucked it up. Let's talk about it.

Could you just call me back already?

Stop sulking and call me back. There are people to save!

"I wish she would just call me back already," Camille said for about the fifth time that week, glancing at the dark screen of her phone.

Rey nodded with all the patience in the world.

Over the last week they had reluctantly—and awkwardly—looked seriously at the finances. The money, once they could actually spend it, would finish off the last of the debts. Between consulting work and her pension, they would be okay even if they occasionally slipped back into old habits. All she had to do was take the job.

"None of this shit would've happened if not for Marcella McKenzie," Camille went on, full of nervous energy but with her head a jumbled mess from her migraine meds. "After all I done for that chipper piece of shit. All the years I've watched her move up the ranks because she's America's goddamn sweetheart. Is she a better cop? No. She's a—a cartoon character. She belongs on a cereal box or a toy commercial, not out on the streets. She should be doing talk shows every day, not sitting behind a desk I should've had a decade ago!"

"Retirement might be nice," Rey said hesitantly. "More time for us. We could go back to that therapist we saw after Ma—after the split. Set some long-term goals for the future."

"The future? Do I even have a future? Thirty-plus years of sitting on my ass, wasting my powers, while these assholes get over with all their guns and their drugs and their trafficking? Blackwell taking over for her boss—it's the same shit in a different toilet, only this time it stinks even more."

"You wouldn't always have to be night shift. We could go on real dates again."

Camille's head snapped up. "Is that what this is about? It's time to get out there again?"

"No, I was thinking we could go dan—"

"Fuck, Rey, I'm too old to be starting over. He left us, he's gone. What's the point of looking again? You go look. I don't care anymore."

Rey grabbed her hands. "Hey. Hey. Don't say that. You care, Cammie. You care too much; that's always been your biggest weakness."

"Who you talking about?" she joked, but her eyes welled up.

"I know he broke your heart, baby, but I'm still right here. It's time to heal and move on. Maybe that means moving on from work, too. To the next step."

She shrugged. "To the next step," she said, like a toast, and stood up, feeling disconnected from her body for the first time in her life.

The drowsiness from the meds had just started to overcome her when the phone finally rang.

"There you are!"

"Sorry, Camille. I got rattled."

"I know you did. That was a tough one. You gonna be alright? You end up with a dope battle scar?"

Vanessa paused. "It was just a scratch. What's up? You have something for us?"

"Don't I always? No arms dealers this time. This job is in my control. The last one wasn't and that's on me."

Vanessa paused again. Rey leaned forward.

"I appreciate you saying that," the kid said in a slow, careful voice that made Camille grit her teeth. "What's the job?"

"I'm working on the details and it'll take a little time to set up. But it's big."

"Big enough to cover my tuition and mortgage?"

"Big enough to retire on *after* you've covered your tuition and mortgage."

"That's awesome."

"You'll be a vet who don't even gotta charge, since after this money ain't a thing. A pro bono veterinarian." Camille laughed.

"I wouldn't mind that, to be honest. When do we start?"

"Like I said, it'll take at least a couple of weeks. But I've got the contract ready and I'm sending it now." Camille pointed to Rey and he clicked a button on the laptop.

"Great. Thanks, Camille."

"Did it come through?"

"One sec...." Vanessa took a little longer than that, and then let out a low sigh. "I got it," she said with her voice more stiff than it even had been.

"You don't like the deal?"

"Fifty-fifty, just like we agreed. What's not to like?" She laughed a little, but Camille didn't buy it.

"You scared? I promise, I'm making a good plan this time, more recon and everything."

"I'll be okay, really, Camille. I can handle it."

"Everyone gets shook," Camille reminded her. "We're human. I suppose." Vanessa did laugh at that. "I'll check in in a few days, alright, kid?"

"Yeah, okay. Later, B."

"Later, kid." Camille disconnected the call with a frown. "Maybe she can't handle it," she said to Rey.

"Well, we planned for that," he said.

Camille's brow furrowed. "Yeah, we did." She headed right for bed. She could barely keep her eyes open. "Rey?"

"Yeah?"

"Call that therapist?"

"Of course, baby."

Chapter 39

Vanessa

I sat out in front of JoMo's Coffee, last paycheck in my bag, and watched for the SUV. Joey had given me a card that he said entitled me to twenty percent off my purchases for life, but also suggested he wouldn't honor it if I didn't help him with the books from time to time. It was a Herculean feat not to roll my eyes at him. I wasn't going to turn down the best coffee in town at a discount, though. And I would absolutely charge him for looking over his books—minus twenty percent, of course.

Camille pulled up, sitting behind the wheel of the SUV. I tensed, even when she rolled down the window with a smile.

"No mo' JoMo?"

I glanced behind me as I opened the passenger door. "I was barely here for a year but it feels like I left a big part of my life behind, you know?"

Camille shrugged. "I mean, you kinda did. This is *the job.* Hey, I noticed you changed your name on the site again. Red Cell, this time? Are you just gonna change your name for each new job?"

"No, I've been thinking a lot about name changes and what direction my future is going. This alias is gonna stick. It's the most appropriate with my powers."

"You and them numbers," she said, shaking her head.

"No Rey today?"

"Nah, he was feeling sick. I told him I'd just drive myself tonight."

"Speaking of which, where are we going?"

Camille didn't blink at the pointed questions. "1023 Bunyan Ave. It's on the edge of the business district, just off the highway."

I cocked my head. "1023 Bunyan? That sounds familiar."

"Yeah, that's because you found it. It was one of the spots you looked up before we ended up at Figgy's Bar this summer."

"One of the Quinn Design & Build construction sites?"

Camille nodded, pleased. "You got it, kid. Good memory."

"You said those weren't great places to do our kind of work. That the stash would be hidden on an overly large plot of land."

"I said what I said. But I've got a friend on the inside who told me exactly where to find what I'm looking for."

"Oh."

Silence fell. We arrived at a secluded construction site on the far edge of town. Turning off the headlights, Camille drove past the parking lot and up a gravel path to the work site. She parked at the edge of the cones and flags that marked off the safety perimeter. Anyone walking further in without a hard hat was risking their own well-being.

The frame was for a small two-story building. One day it would be filled with medical facilities, but right then, there weren't even any walls. The site consisted of girders, wooden slats for floors, a few completed stairways, and an unfinished concrete foundation. Camille led the way up a wide set of stairs to the second floor.

"This isn't our kind of business, Camille."

"Yeah, we discussed that on the way." She gave me a look that told me to keep up while she continued forward.

"What I'm saying is that the other places we hit were actively funneling money in and shipping it out. There was a fluctuating count."

"Okay," she responded, seemingly annoyed by the topic.

"If this is just a stash in an unattended area, we aren't busting up anything. We're just taking. Not counting, not fighting, just taking."

"You're smart. Had you been a bit smarter, you'd have said all this back in the car. Or smarter still, over the phone before accepting the contract. Come take a look at something." Camille walked to the edge of the incomplete second floor and looked over to the ground level we'd just left. She indicated that I should look down as well.

The only thing visible in the low-light was the unfinished foundation. The most recent pour of cement didn't appear set and a mixer was positioned nearby, slowly turning a fresh batch. As I leaned forward to have a look, I felt Camille behind me and took a step back.

"This isn't a score. Why did you bring me here, Camille?"

"You ain't already guessed?"

"I have. But I want to hear you say it."

Camille sighed. "Turns out, all this work we been putting in together turned into an even bigger audition for the both of us. I passed mine. Yours is still undecided."

I worked hard to keep my cool. "What are you talking about?"

"I've been recruited as part of a, let's say, reorganization effort by one of the crime families that we hit. Tomorrow, I start as a consultant on police placements and strategy. There's room for a top-notch accountant. I'll *make* room for a top-notch accountant. But you've got to agree. Right here. Right now. It's either this," she said as she gestured over the edge "...or that. So, what's it going to be?"

Chapter 40

Camille

"So, this is how you want it to be?" Vanessa asked.

Camille couldn't read the kid's expression. "It's not what I want it to be. It's just how it *is*. This is all a business and you gotta look out for self. You know too much about my off-the-script activities. Either we've got to maintain our partnership or end it permanently."

Vanessa took a moment before speaking. "Y'know, I was warned that you'd turn on me."

"Who'd you talk to about me?" Camille jolted back, surprised. Was there someone else in the picture she had to take care of? The thought exhausted her. Why wouldn't the kid just take the deal? Maybe the pitch left something to be desired, but it was a good deal. Lucrative for them both.

"This jazzman I met at a local nightspot. Do you know Mateo? He told me you were the worst at partnerships, that you'd use me until it wasn't convenient, then discard me." Rage and pain welled up in her, overwhelming her. She opened her mouth to respond, but the kid kept talking.

"You know what else he said? He said that as bad of a partner as you were, you're an even worse superhero. Always chasing after fame instead of letting good work stand on its own.

"I can see what he meant, too. You had all those successful takedowns of crime spots. But you only did that for the fast money. If you had that same energy for your legit job, Pierce wouldn't just be a safer neighborhood, it would be a utopia. I guess not everybody can be Double M, right?"

"You shut your damn mouth." She was fuming. Was the kid playing her, or did Mateo really think all that about her? He'd never said anything, but he didn't need to. He was all sad eyes and disappointment. Always disappointed. She could either hate herself or get mad, so she'd gotten mad, as mad as she was now.

"Shut my damn mouth or what? You'll do what you came here to do anyway? I guess that's it for me then, but between your precinct, your husbands, and your partnership with me, I'm wondering why Teresa Blackwell even thinks she can count on you. But I guess the counting has always been *my* job."

The kid knew. The kid *was* playing her! Her, Camille Baston, B-Girl!

"Count on this! Numbers aren't gonna save you this time. Jump in or I'll throw you in. Your choice."

But the kid was cool as ice. "Our powers aren't too different," she said mildly.

It almost made her laugh. "That's funny, people keep trying to tell me how we're *so* much alike. Our powers are nothing alike, kid."

"Aren't they, though? When you boil it all the way down, we're both readers. If you give us enough information to read, we can pick up on things that normals can't."

"You getting to a point, or...?"

"What I read is the reason you suck as a hero. It's because you treat it like an entitlement instead of a vocation." Vanessa walked straight towards her. Camille, confused, took a few steps back. "Your only purpose is yourself. You don't have the heart for this. Not really. Maybe you never have. You're not a hero. You're just an opportunist, an underemployed mercenary, just one more leech on a society that's already full of them." Vanessa closed the gap and poked Camille at the top of her jumpsuit.

"Okay, fuck you. In you go." But they'd moved too far from the edge. The only option was a fight.

Camille launched her right fist at Vanessa's face. Vanessa moved out of the way easily. The left fist followed and Vanessa dodged that, too—and the next one and the next one.

"H-how are you doing this?" Camille cried in desperation. She threw another two punches, fast as she could, but it was like the kid could read her mind.

And then she was on the ground.

Three people in black tactical gear tackled her and pinned her to the floor. Where had they come from? She put up a struggle, but between the rage and frustration, she was spent, and her powers couldn't respond to something that had already happened. A few seconds later, she was flat on her stomach with zip-ties on her wrists and ankles.

A young man who didn't look familiar at all stood next to Vanessa.

Vanessa crouched low enough to address Camille in a smooth, conversational voice. "It's like I said. Give us enough info and we can tell where the story is going before it gets there. Most people can't see my powers, and when they do they think it's about numbers. It isn't. It's about trends. And you throw the same punch combination in the same order. Every single time."

Chapter 41

Vanessa

"So, what now? You a killer now? The government looks into it when a client dies before the contract gets closed out. You 'bout to go to jail for the rest of your life."

I shook my head at her. "You're not my client, Camille. Rey's my client. That's why this contract popped up under some miscellaneous new client ID, and that's why Rey's mysteriously sick tonight. Contractors can't kill their clients, but clients can't kill their contractors either. You came out here to kill me and you had to make sure he couldn't be implicated in my death. He's probably out having a drink somewhere public with a lot of cameras."

Camille pulled against the zip ties to no avail. "So what then, smart girl? You know if you don't kill me, I'm just gonna get up and kill you."

I looked down at her face, taking her in. I had cared about her. I still did, really, even though she was a scary mess. She only knew how to be angry. Even her sadness looked more like anger than anything else. And while I'd been harsh, I didn't think I'd been off the mark.

"I'm sorry I was so mean, Camille. I had to get you off your game—distracted and reckless. And I did think about you wanting revenge. All the advice I got says that I *should* dump you in the same cement bath you meant for me. But I can't do that. I don't want to. Instead, I'm going to go the other way." I nodded at Bobby and he crouched down as well, drawing her attention.

"Who the fuck are you?"

"I'm Bobby. Vanessa's boyfriend. Pleased to make your acquaintance." He looked from Camille to me and asked, "You sure about this? It can backfire in a lot of ways."

"I know what I want, Bobby. Make it happen." I was trying really hard to ignore the "boyfriend" part for now. I had to keep it together. Without this next part going exactly right, I would be a dead girl walking.

"Okay." Bobby sighed, unlocked his phone, and dialed a number neither Camille nor I could see. "It's me. Do it. Yeah, just like we talked about."

"What the hell is going on here? Do what?"

"Oh, I guess I could be a bit clearer," he said, ending the call. "My name is Robert Quinn, Jr. This is my building and this is my outfit. You know, the one you just tried and failed to take down? As you can imagine, this enterprise is quite wealthy. So, we've arranged for a single payment of fifteen million dollars to be made to an offshore account in your name. Your half of this job's commission, split evenly between the two contractors."

Pulling out my own phone, I swiped over to the drafted email I had prepared a few hours ago and hit Send. "I'm forwarding you the account details and instructions on how to access it right now, Camille."

"What the fuck are you talking about? I'm not an operator."

"No, you're not," I said. "But now *you've* got a choice to make. You can act up and Bobby's people will make it look like you accepted off-contract work. That would make you a rogue. Your previous busts, including all the work we did together, would get scrutinized. You'd be labeled a multiple offender and go to prison. That's a minimum of eight years, but knowing your reputation among your law enforcement colleagues, you'll probably get the maximum of twenty-five. *Or* you can get in your car, go home to Rey, and retire comfortably on the fifteen mil your partner just helped you earn.

"Also, please know that I recorded all of this from the point I got in your car up to right now. I'll be keeping a copy of the audio file real safe in case you ever change your mind about coming after me. A tough pill to swallow, I know. But with the money and your newly-revived public image, it's basically everything you ever wanted. It's better than you deserve, and I think you'll find a way to fuck it up. But I could never forgive myself if I let Bobby handle this the way he wanted to."

Camille practically snarled. "That's really not much of a choice."

I shrugged. "I know, and being beat by a 'kid' who can't fight has gotta suck. But sometimes it's tough, Camille. Sometimes the job ain't pretty."

"Cute. You win, V-Girl."

"Red Cell. *That's* my name." I smiled. It fit just right.

I looked at Bobby, who nodded at his three men. Two unholstered their weapons and kept them trained on Camille as the third produced a knife and cut her free. Rubbing her wrists, she stood up and made one final assessment of her situation before giving a nod to me and walking towards the stairs.

"Hey B!" I called out. "Mateo didn't say any of that stuff, you know that, right? I was just trying to rile you up." She stopped, and it was like all the anger dropped out of her body, leaving only sadness.

"Good to know," she said in a voice so low it took me a second to register the words.

And then she descended the stairs and disappeared out of my life.

Bobby's people followed her in case her resignation was an act, leaving the two of us alone. I let out the biggest breath in the universe.

"Oh my god! I was terrified through all of that. How did I sound? Did I sound cool?"

"Very," he said, putting his arm around me and grinning. "You were like an action star."

I grinned back but my knees were still weak. "Oh shit—but what about Teresa? Did you catch her?"

"No, but I wasn't exactly expecting to. Her ability to spot and evade traps is unreal. She made my guys from a distance and took off before we even had a chance to close in. She's out of the game now, though, and she has to know it."

"Well, in that case, at least you were able to save your dad." He didn't respond. "Your dad," I said again. "If Teresa bolted then she didn't get to your dad."

Everything clicked into place, but I didn't want to believe it. I pulled away and looked up at him.

"Vanessa..." he said, looking pained. "We didn't try to spring the trap until Teresa was leaving my father's office. Her next stop would've been here to help B-Girl with you. That would've tipped the odds."

"But—you could've sprung the trap earlier! You were supposed to stop her from hurting your dad!"

He paused, and then said quietly, "I never said I was going to do that."

I couldn't even speak.

"Crime is inevitable," he said. "You see the trends even better than I do. You've helped to reduce the harm, but there was no way you were going to end crime completely. If my father and his organization didn't exist, someone else would come along."

"But... you?"

"Why not me? I'm certainly a better choice than Blackwell. At least this way it's someone who actually cares."

"Yeah, because crime bosses are really known for harm reduction. You could end all this right now. But you're not going to."

"I'm not," he agreed. "I earned this."

"You said you were my boyfriend," I said, unable to stop the words from coming out. I heard the whine in them, which made me want to jump in the cement myself.

"I want to be," he said. "I'm serious about caring, and not just about the organization, but the organization *will* change under me. There won't be any more trafficking. Nothing without consent.

"I'm not going to threaten you like Camille did. If you walk, that's it. I'll respect that, and I believe you'll respect me and give me a chance to do better than my father. Am I right, Vanessa?"

I looked at his face, those stunning blue eyes, and I ran the numbers. I held that handsome face in my hands, and I kissed him.

"I believe you," I told him, "but I can't be with you."

And then I walked.

Sorry, Stephen.

Chapter 42

Camille

Camille drove restlessly around the city. She didn't know if Rey was home yet or what she would tell him when she saw him. She didn't know where Teresa Blackwell was or if she was even still alive. Her mind raced, so she just let her SUV race as well.

Worse than that, she felt a migraine coming on and she didn't have her meds on hand. The only thing worse than having a severe headache was driving with one. So, she found a spot to park in a familiar neighborhood, reclined the driver's seat as far back as possible, and fell asleep, hoping for a clearer mind upon awakening.

What she got was the pleasant aroma of coffee and crisp fall air through the vehicle's open window. The early-morning sunshine gave Camille an indication of how long she had slept. It only took a slight turn of her head to see that she had landed outside of JoMo Java. Months had passed since her last caramel drizzle latte. Going home made more sense, but she felt compelled to head inside.

The door chimed as Camille entered. The place was empty without the weekday work crowd. The only exception was the owner, who looked up to greet her.

"First customer on a Saturday, Camille? That's a surprise. If you're looking for Van, she quit a while back. She actually just picked up her final paycheck last night."

"Nah. I... already saw Vanessa." It had been a mostly agreeable two minutes from the time Camille woke up until the impact of the last twelve hours kicked in. What was done was done though, and what Camille needed was clarity about the things that had yet to be done. "I want to ask you something, Joey. Fix me my usual?"

"You got it. What do you wanna know?" JoMo turned to fix the drink with practiced ease. He really was good at this part of his job.

"Back in the day, I sent you up. When you got out of jail, you started stealing again and I damn near sent you up a second time. I chose not to. Realistically, you could've gone right back to thieving after that. Instead you opened up this shop. Why?" In all the years that she had access to this man and this shop, she had never thought to ask this before. Today, though, she needed an answer.

"Honestly? When you caught me the first time, I didn't have any skills. I wasn't a hardened criminal. I was a kid with nothing better happening and robbing houses brought in easy money. When you caught me the second time, I realized that I didn't have that excuse anymore. I learned how to make coffee on the inside. The vocational rehabilitation program, y'know. I could've gone for the easy money again but it would've put me back in the same place. Coffee money is a lot harder to get, but I can spend it."

249

Camille could tell that her old classmate took pride in his craft. It was something she wished she could've been doing for the last thirty-two years. Maybe it was too late. Maybe not. Either way, she couldn't stand still anymore.

"I feel that. Thanks, Joey. Take care of yourself." She dropped a ten dollar bill on the counter and returned to her car.

The drive across town didn't take long, but Camille stalled before entering the precinct. Though she told herself she was just finishing her drink, she knew she was steeling herself for what came next. The finished latte took away her last excuse and she left her SUV in the lot. After a brief stop by her mostly-empty locker, she headed to her captain's office.

With the door open as usual, Camille could hear the sounds of an urgent news report as she approached.

An out-of-control operator may be responsible for the murder of lobbyist John Christopher Hale, the kidnapping of medical expert Kani Sidana, and an explosion that's left the Washington Four Seasons Hotel severly damaged. We are awaiting the release of the extralegal operations contract information that may be the key to understanding how these events came to pass. North American News will keep you informed as details about the ongoing investigation come in.

Double M had a pained expression on her face when she noticed Camille standing in her door frame. "Have you seen this, Baston?"

"No, what is it?" Stepping in, she glanced at the television and saw the fiery wreck that used to be a room in a luxury hotel.

"They're saying an operator exploded a D.C. hotel room while on a job. That's a lot of collateral damage, for sure, but the news keeps saying 'murder' and 'kidnapping' as if those weren't part of the job. Meanwhile, they're moving real slow on releasing the contract info. You know what that sounds like?"

"It sounds like a rogue. Between this one and the one Fish took down a few months back, that's not a good look for operators in general."

"You're not wrong. Technically, rogues aren't even really operators. Without a contract, they're just out of control superhumans. Almost nobody makes that distinction though. Operators are gonna catch hell for this. Funny thing is, the kidnapped woman? She's someone I knew from way back when." Double M's voice stiffened. Her eyes went glassy for a moment before Camille brought her back to the present.

"Another one of your *'rumored'* girlfriends, huh?" Camille put up air quotes. The Captain glared before exhaling and sitting up straighter in her seat.

"Hmph. Can I help you with something, Camille, or did you just pop by on your day off to be an asshole?"

Camille came farther into the office and closed the door behind her. She reached into her pocket and pulled out a badge. She hadn't actually worn it on her person in decades. Even stowed away in her locker, though, it was... symbolic.

"This is what you wanted, isn't it?" She flung the badge on the desk as she sat down opposite her captain. M caught it on a bounce.

251

"Just like that? No yelling? No fanfare? I gave you until the end of the year. You've got almost three months left. I could arrange a farewell party or something."

"Why? So Morella can smile in my face and thank me for my exemplary service? So people like Fish and Avon can pretend to be sad I'm leaving? Fuck that. It's over, M. There's nothing left for me here." Even as she said it, Camille felt a huge weight leave her shoulders. She hadn't even realized she had been carrying it. But with nothing left to prove and no one else to work for, she was as unburdened as she'd been since first leaving Hawkins to be a big-city cop.

The Captain looked puzzled. "What will you do now? I don't take you for a 'sit on the couch watching soap operas' type." Camille shrugged.

"I don't really know yet. I'm gonna talk it over with my husband and see what we come up with."

Double M placed her hands on the desk in front of her. She looked genuinely concerned.

"Can I make a suggestion?"

"Ha! I've got nothing but free time to hear it."

"I don't know what kind of dirt you were into. But what you did on that boat for those trafficking victims was something real. Most of them, the ones who wanted it, received asylum here in the U.S. And what you said on the news about decriminalizing sex work resonated with some of the local politicians. Maybe you wanna do something with that? You only just rebuilt your public platform in the last few months. It'd be a shame to see it all go to waste."

"That's definitely something to think about." An awkward silence fell between them. The second Camille left this room, she knew the ride would be over. Suddenly, she wasn't as enthusiastic about getting out of her chair. She grasped at a reason to stay a little longer. "So, did you want to know what kind of dirt I was into... allegedly?"

M laughed. "Absolutely! I love a good story and hearing yours sounds better than everything else that's going on with me."

"Well, back in April, I met this young–" The ringing of Double M's phone interrupted. M's eyebrows creased when she saw the number on the phone's display.

"Give me a second. I've gotta take this. Hey Maxie! Of course. I was just watching it on the news. Are you involved? Give me a second."

Double M put the phone on mute and stood up. "I'm sorry, Cam. Something major is about to go down and this call may take a while. Can I get a raincheck on the story? I haven't forgotten that you still owe me that drink."

"Sure, let's get together when things calm down for you. I know the perfect place." Camille extended her hand and Double M took it. Amazing how easy it was to be civil when the stakes were completely off the table.

"I'm sorry it went down this way. Truly. But I'm glad you're leaving on top. Vets deserve classy exits and no one out there," she said, and motioned towards the door and the rest of the precinct "...will ever know it was anything but."

Camille nodded and reached for the door knob. "I appreciate that, McKenzie."

"Be good, B-Girl," she replied, with a flip of her trademark purple hair.

"Ain't I always?" Camille shot back as she left. Over her shoulder, she heard Double M resume her conversation.

"I'm back, Max. I'll need details, but I can be down there as soon as you need me."

Hearing her voice fade away into the background seemed appropriate for Camille. Also appropriate? Ignoring every other human on her way out of the building. By the time she reached her car, she was completely ready to leave it all behind.

Chapter 43

Vanessa

So now what?

That was the question. B-Girl hadn't been kidding when she said this money could set me up for life, especially with my head for numbers. I could do anything.

I could do nothing.

I could get my own place, pretty dresses, amazing kicks, and a huge TV where I could play video games and watch basketball all day. Honestly, only a few months ago I would have said that was the dream. Nowadays, it sounded kinda empty.

As a teenager, I'd had many goals, almost all of which revolved around basketball. I watched them all be taken from me by what I thought was nothing more than bad timing. But maybe Malik was right. I was a variant, and that wasn't something you could turn off for the games.

Maybe it was obvious to everyone but me, but I'd definitely fallen into, at best, a slump... at worst, a depression. I could see it clearly now that I was past it.

"Van?"

First things first. That fucking name.

I stood up from my spot on the driveway under the basketball hoop. "I don't think that's my name, Dad."

He stepped out of the front door and looked at me seriously, and I finally saw it: even when I didn't know I was depressed, he did. He wasn't a psychologist, just a dad doing his best. Sometimes his best was hurtful or annoying. But he loved me. He really did.

Which is why I didn't want to lie to him anymore.

"Vanessa."

"I don't think that's it either," I told him, looking at him dead on. "I tried to keep an in-between name. I really did. But it feels wrong. It feels... itchy."

There was a long silence. Even when your dad backs your play ninety-nine percent of the time, you wait for that one percent, because that's the part that comes at you like a knife.

Or maybe I wasn't giving him enough credit. I took a deep breath and let it out. With it went some of my tension. If he didn't approve, so what? Hadn't I proven myself? My actual self, whatever her name was?

"You have something else in mind?" he finally asked, and there went the rest of my tension.

"Not yet," I told him. "But I'm gonna give it some thought. Just like everything else. No hasty decisions. Except maybe season tickets for the Gizmos."

He grinned. "Maybe one for your dad too?"

"Of course. No more ragging on Taylor, though."

He held up his hands. "She gets the job done, I have to admit."

"Yeah," I said, grinning back. "She does."

"I'll leave you to it," he said, and went back in the house. I swore I could already smell popcorn.

Money doesn't buy happiness, but it buys stability. With stability there's a lot more wiggle room for happiness. I turned over numbers in my head, thought about looking up patterns in the housing market. But my mind kept coming back to wondering what did make me happy.

I knew that helping people made me happy, or at least fulfilled. It was something I first learned day after day serving coffee at JoMo's, but that happiness wasn't the same as finding embezzlers and bringing down sex trafficking rings. I wasn't really built for staring down criminals with guns, though. That was for people with powers like B-Girl or Double M.

I knew in my heart I wasn't ready to delete my operator profile. But I also didn't want to make it my life. I wanted to find somewhere that I was the best person for the job and be that best person. So the profile was going to stay.

And then I had a really silly idea. The kind of idea you'd forget about in an instant if you didn't happen to have silly amounts of money.

Dogs.

Don't get me wrong—I was going to have a net, or even a court, at my next place. I was going to invite Malik, and we were going to play. I was going to jump online before bed and shoot monsters and machines in video games with my friends. I was definitely going to get at least two dogs. But those things weren't going to help anyone. Well, except maybe the dogs.

An animal rescue, on the other hand, would.

Was it a pipe dream? Yeah, maybe, but the more I thought about it (and then looked it up online), the more I thought it was something I could make happen. I'd need help. A vet, for sure. But you know who else was necessary for something like that?

A lawyer.

I looked down at my phone. Her name was still there. I knew I probably didn't have a chance to make things right in a romantic sense, and that was okay. If it came up, I'd shoot my shot. But if it didn't, it didn't. This wasn't about me, or us.

This was about all the dogs we could help.

Still, I didn't call yet. I had a lot of planning to do, houses to hunt, and season tickets to purchase.

And a dad to have dinner with.

Chapter 44

Camille

"I want to thank you all for coming here today."

Robert Quinn, Jr. wore an expensive dark suit, had an expensive haircut, looked every bit the mourning son. Camille could almost believe he cared, if she didn't think that maybe he was the reason Blackwell wasn't returning her calls. "It's a testament to my father's life to see St. Andrew's filled with people whose lives he touched." *And those are just the ones who are clean enough to show their faces*, Camille thought.

"This was the scene this morning at St. Andrew's this morning in downtown Cargill," a reporter said, as the scene changed from shaky phone footage to a news camera set outside the cathedral. "Robert Quinn, Sr., was a beloved boss, a beloved friend, and a man known around Cargill and its suburbs for driving a hard deal, but he always made time to better the community. His last major project before his death at fifty-eight from cancer, Homes for the Homeless, was spearheaded by his son, Robert Jr., known by most as Bobby, and it's to Bobby the keys to the Quinn Design & Build empire have gone."

"Who writes this shit?" Camille asked Rey.

"The people with the money," Rey said. "TV station probably gets a script stapled to a bag full of cash."

"Yeah," she said, tilting her head, and watched the scene cut back to Bobby's pretty, empty words. She wished she had Vanessa's power to see how this would all go. Not only Bobby and the organization. Her and Rey, too. Would they fuck it up again? Could she and Rey make a real future together, one without scrambling and always failing? "Tomorrow morning, I'm setting up a meeting with a financial planner."

Without taking his eyes off the screen, her husband leaned nearer and replied, "Smart. I'll come with you. Maybe I'll learn something new."

Camille reached out and took his hand. As always, his grasp was firm. He squeezed, and she felt a flood of relief for this one person who always stood by her.

"I love you," she said.

"I love you too, baby."

She turned off the TV.

Chapter 45

Aurora

I stretched out on my fabulous new couch. My two new doggos, named after the greatest heroes in the greatest video game series of all time, were conked out next to me after an exhausting game of Destroy Every Dog Toy Known To Humankind. I would have to hit up the pet store again tomorrow. Not that I had a problem with that.

I picked up my phone and hit the call button.

"Vanessa?"

"Hey, Elise."

"Wow! It's been a while. I wasn't expecting to hear from you again. Are you okay?" I only heard concern in her voice, not anger or annoyance. That was a good sign.

"I am. Better than okay, actually. I'm sorry I ghosted. I've been going through a lot lately. Most of it good, though. Can I tell you about some of it?"

"I guess. I've got a little time to talk."

"Sorry, I didn't mean right this moment. How about tomorrow night?"

"Tomorrow night?" She laughed. "Can't. You know the season starts tomorrow, right? I'll be planted in front of my TV."

"I figured. But I've got two courtside tickets to the Gizmos' season opener. I could use a date. If you're interested."

"Courtside at the season opener? Are you kidding? Of course I'm interested! How did you get tickets?"

"I actually have season tickets a few sections up from the court. But these particular tickets were gifted to me by 'Break-of-Dawn' Taylor herself."

"Oh my god! There really *is* a story here. I don't want to hear some of it, I want to hear all of it."

"Awesome. I'll pick you up tomorrow at six then."

"I can't wait. But speaking of wanting to hear it all... you never told me you used to play seriously, Vanessa." Called it. "I was flipping through the Summer League record books down at the rec center. Your name is in there *a lot*."

"It should be. I was pretty fantastic back then. Oh, and thanks for the heads up. I'll need to ask them to update those records. I'm going by Aurora now." It felt amazing every time I said it.

"That's a beautiful name. Text me tomorrow morning to confirm?"

"Will do. I'm really looking forward to seeing you, Elise."

Her voice lowered, warmed. "Me too, Aurora."

About the Authors

Kevin Patterson, M.Ed has been practicing ethical nonmonogamy since 2002. In 2015, Kevin was inspired to start Poly Role Models, a popular interview series blog. The blog extended into speaking engagements about how race and polyamory intersect and the writing of his award-winning book "Love's Not Color Blind." Kevin has since poured his efforts into writing goofy, queer superhero novels. You're holding one.

Alana Phelan is a librarian, writer, editor, and community organizer. She lives in South Jersey with her family, many cats, and a surprisingly large Dorbz collection. You can find her online as The Polyamorous Librarian, where she writes an advice column and offers workshops and relationship support.

Where can you find us?

For Hire

Facebook.com/ForHireMag

Twitter: @ForHireMag

Kevin A. Patterson

Facebook.com/PolyRoleModels

PolyRoleModels.tumblr.com

Patreon.com/PolyRoleModels

Twitter/Instagram: @PolyRoleModels

YouTube: Poly Role Models

PolyRoleModels@gmail.com

Alana Phelan

PolyamorousLibrarian.wordpress.com

Facebook.com/PolyamorousLibrarian

Twitter: @HelloLibrarian

Patreon.com/PolyamorousLibrarian

Acknowledgements

We couldn't have made this launch run as smoothly and as successfully as it has without a ton of support from the people who backed us on IndieGoGo! Endless appreciation and we hope you loved the book!

Crystal Summons • Andraya B Copass • Angela Rauscher • Patrick Gudat • Aimee M Moran • Liz Powell • Josh Hanson • Kristie Flournoy • Gabor Laszlo • Polina Litvak • Jerliyah Craig • Jess Tetro • Dominique Theodore Thomas • Rak Doering • Lee Soeburn • Julia Clark • Red Lhota • Ky Putnam • Mario Garza III • Bernard Gray • Saga Lowe • Manjari Olds • Ashlei Perry • Imani Thomas • Marcus Gonzales • Ray Henry • Rachael Brunner • Kit M Rowland • Kate Jack Ferenczi • Nathaniel Victor Preston • Nathan Weyer • John Morella • Heather Cellini • Sean Holmes • Amanda Barr-Orlandini • Derrick Laning • Brandon Oglesby • Erika Kapin • Tammy Cravit • Wendy Sheridan • Heather Fox • Mary Jones • Robyn Giles • Myra Williams • Kate Rivera • Obermeier Electric • Robin Renee • Katrina Douglass • Di Schempp • Melinda Graham • Felicia Upshaw • Al Campbell • Barbara White • Eve Rickert • Devlin Mckee • Kevin Hogan • Krista Haapala • Stephen Wright Jr • Holly Freundlich

Made in the USA
Monee, IL
21 December 2019